I0647068

Gora
And Other Dark Narratives

Gora

And Other Dark Narratives

by

Daegal

CASTLE
CARRINGTON

Castle Carrington Publishing

Perceptions
Press

an imprint of
Perceptions Press
Victoria, BC, Canada

2024

Gora
And Other Dark Narratives

Copyright © Daegal 2024

All rights reserved. No part of this publication may be reprinted, reproduced, stored in a retrieval system, or transmitted in any form or by any means, electronic, mechanical, photocopying and recording, or otherwise, now known or hereafter invented without the express prior written permission of the author, except for brief passages quoted by a reviewer in a newspaper or magazine. To perform any of the above is an infringement of copyright law.

No AI training. Without in any way limiting the author's [and publisher's] exclusive rights under copyright, any use of this publication to "train" generative artificial intelligence (AI) technologies to generate text is expressly prohibited. The author reserves all rights to license uses of this work for generative AI training and development of machine learning language models.

This is a work of fiction. Names, characters, places, events, locales, and incidents are either the products of the author's imagination or used in a fictitious manner. Any resemblance to actual persons, living or dead, or actual events is purely coincidental.

First published in paperback in 2024

Cover Art and Design: Daegal
Illustrations: Daegal

ISBN: 978-1-998924-79-0 (paperback)
ISBN: 978-1-998924-80-6 (Kindle-e-book)
ISBN: 978-1-998924-81-3 (Smashwords/Draft2Digital e-book)

Published in Canada by
Castle Carrington Publishing
www.castlecarringtonpublishing.ca

a Division of
Perceptions Press
www.perceptionspress.ca
Victoria, BC Canada

CASTLE
CARRINGTON

Perceptions
Press

Contents

Part 1

DARK NARRATIVES

Gora

The transcription of this diary is fiction and intended as such. It does not refer to real characters or to actual events. Any likeness to the living or dead is purely coincidental. Maybe.

"You should reconsider the flower beds."

I circled the spoon, watching the cream swirl, turning the coffee caramel. I couldn't drink it black. It wasn't delightful, and it made my tongue burn.

"It's acidic, Sister," she would preach.

Gora loved to preach. The unnecessary sermon fell on deaf ears.

"It's why I don't drink that poison," she would continue, giving me the once over.

It was habitual behavior, and I always nodded, letting Gora feel inclined.

"Well," "I raised my teacup, hovering it above my bottom lip. "Mother would have liked us to continue the upkeep, don't you think?"

Sister blew a puff of air from her bottom lip and nodded, folding her hands over her belly. We started every day in the living room, lounging in our nightgowns, with myself perched on the edge of the couch, and Gora lying across the loveseat. Sister shifted her elbows under her weight, leaned up, wiggled her feet back and forth, and looked at the ceiling.

"I am not opposed to cleaning the garden." She craned her neck and gave me an exhausted look. "But," she paused to make a point, "I have no desire to maintain the upkeep."

I sipped my coffee and then cleared my throat. Gora knew my tactics. There would be a sob followed by some language of understanding and then my resounding, "But..."

She hated the subtle conflict I would drum up when concerning our parents. There was no conflict. They were dead. They left two children with significant traumas to fend for themselves. It was selfish.

We were born in 1902—identical twins. The monozygotic, not fraternal or the dizygotic, kind. Father said we were exceptional and spent hours reading about us in his private library. We were never allowed in there, ever. When he learned something new, he would barge into the living room, interrupting all conversations to announce his findings. I recall one instance where I thought my father had lost his sensibility.

"Galton" he raised his finger, pausing for dramatic effect.

When we stared at him, oblivious, he dropped his hand, slumped his shoulders, and furrowed his bushy eyebrows.

"Galton," he repeated. "Francis Galton?"

We never really knew who this man was, but we pretended to.

"He studied eugenics," Father exclaimed. "And he's British."

That was the most critical part of the man's credibility—he was British. We shook our heads, feigning interest.

Mother praised, "That's good, dear," as she walked away.

Father scoffed, mumbling as he returned to his library, slamming the door behind him.

I looked out the big bay window to the yard and took a deep breath. Turning to Gora, I straightened my posture to look more assertive.

"What if I tend to the trillium and the blue flag and you to Father's cherry blossoms?"

Gora sat up and straightened her nightgown. There was the, 'But…'"

I could tell she didn't want to tend to any of it.

"Fine," she sulked and lowered herself back down. She draped her forearm over her eyes and let out a moan.

"Stop being so dramatic, Sister." I laughed, picking up the saucer and walking into the kitchen, leaving Gora to pout.

It was June and already stifling outside. It was our birthday on the 5th, and neither of us has mentioned a word of it so far. Ever since our parents had passed, holidays seemed unimportant and, more so, birthdays. What was there to celebrate? Sure, we had no worries about monetary struggles, but the most important people who gave us life were gone. They left us with nothing but heartache, mental illness, and a beautiful prison by which to remember them. That was hardly a good reason to blow out candles.

I placed my cup and saucer in the sink and stood in the vast empty kitchen. I could smell the ghost of my mother. Was it Mother? The loaves of bread and pastries that Mother slaved over for Father hung at the end of my flared nostrils. So, yes, it was Mother. Sometimes, when I walked the halls at night, I could hear Mother singing from empty rooms at the far ends of the mansion, always wherever I was not.

Downstairs, the smell of Father's pipe leaked from behind the library door. I did not dare to open it. Not wanting to see his rotten corpse sitting upright in the leather chair, smoke curling his gaunt face.

"Galton!" he would squawk, pulling the pipe from his twisted mouth, the teeth decayed and spare. This place was our tomb.

My sister and I suffered from agoraphobia. Father had lectured us on the subject, and, for a short period, we paid attention. He said it was related to a panic disorder. Still, neither my sister nor I ever felt any panic unless you asked us to leave the boundaries of our property. The condition, discovered by Karl Friedrich Otto Westphal, was not easily dissuaded. Father took him as a serious and notable doctor of psychiatry, even though he was German and not British.

My sister and I never understood the difference between the two, so we focused on the information rather than the heritage of the scholar. There were moments when we dared each other to cross the property's boundaries. If memory serves correctly, we both had stepped one toe over the line. The fear climbed us like old vines, threatening to pull us under the earth. We would squeal and run back into the protection of our home. The cool brick walls sealed us from the outside world, its cold grip hugging our forms. Nothing could be touched within its frigid shell. Not in a harmful way, at least.

Father would scold us as we ran through the living room, screeching and bellowing as if creatures nipped at our heels. They did. I swore to my sister, in whom I confided on my accounts of these matters, and she, in turn, spun equal tales of the heel biters. I assure you, they were real, but Sister thought we conjured all of them from fear. Apparitions within our imaginations. Purely fun. Fantasy to excite the mundane. The fable had natural teeth, and I have the marks to prove it.

I would bear another scar in the summer of our twenty-third birthday. My sister would call me a "spinster of lies" and rush to the yard's border to prove her discord. Everything changed that afternoon when she returned from the yard's edge. It was not the last time I would hear her voice, however. Several days would pass before she would sing to me.

But I am getting ahead of myself. Let me back up a moment and share what happened to my sister. It is all written down. The day she decided to leave us. I write in this diary from the depths of our home. In the shadows, neither my sister, mother, nor father can know my thoughts, but they hear me.

Oh, by the way, my name is Phoebe.

June 5th Diary Entry

It was inconceivable to think that Gora would do what she did. That morning, we took tea in the living room and pretended to have forgotten what day it was. I had made Gora a modest gift—a puffed pastry topped with fresh honey. I got stung a few times and considered that an acceptable sacrifice to please my sister on the day we agreed not to celebrate. I had no idea if she had planned something on my behalf, but from the smile on her face, I assumed it was as equally deliberate. It was beautiful outside. The sun stabbed through the trees and illuminated the green carpet of the yard.

I wanted to lay in it, and my skin prickled with excitement. Gora stuck her hand straight up and made circles with her pointer finger. Why is she so weird sometimes? I remember sighing just then. Not because I felt annoyed or bored. It was as if I knew what came next—a clairvoyance of heavy sorrow that my sister exuded. I don't know. These things are best left to the imagination, or so I thought.

I stood, dragged my feet to the bay window, and watched the outside world as if in a dream. Gora continued to paint the ceiling, humming "Itsy Bitsy Spider." It was very immature for her age, but somehow, the song fit the moment—something in the way it vibrated from her chest, like the wailing of a small child. Creepy. A hummingbird zipped across the window, and I jumped back, placing my hand across my chest.

"My heavens," I laughed.

I looked at Gora, signaling for her to come and see. Sister dropped her arm, letting it hang by her side, and looked into the backside of the cushion. She is so dramatic. I ignored her negative behavior and returned my gaze to the little visitor. It had hovered above a batch of black and blue salvia. It ducked its beak in and out, pausing to ensure I was a spectator.

By the way, those beaks are called maxilla, and they are flexible. But we are not here for an ornithology lesson, so I will add one last thing about the little visitor before we continue. I could hear the faint buzz of its invisible wings, which made my heart joyful. It would be the last time joy that feral would fill my heart and aura. Something else would come to fill those spaces, but again, I am rushing.

I went to Gora and cupped her hand, biting my bottom lip.

"Let us try the border, Sister!" I teased.

Her head rolled, the hair cascading over her big blue eyes. She looked like a beautiful corpse, pale and pristine. Her lips parted into a cute pout as words seeped from her palate.

"No," she turned her head back around.

I dropped her hand, and I remember feeling a kind of disdain, close to hate, as I stared at the back of her head.

"Why are you always so melancholy, Sister?"

Something changed then. I could not place my finger on the causation, but Gora jumped and parted her hair. Her eyes were wide and bright, her teeth clenched.

"To the yard, then," she sneered and, grabbing my wrist, dragged me to the front door.

Gora flung the front doors open, and the sun threw daggers into our eyes. We recoiled simultaneously as if the duality of our reflexes was intentional, an inner warning that fell upon the ignorant bliss of excitement. Looking back, I see it now, but isn't that everyone's recollection of these circumstances? Gora bounced down the stairs leaving me to shield my eyes.

"Now, don't take any wooden nickels, Sister!"

She looked back only once as she headed toward the property's border. I held my breath and extended my hand as if to caution her. The heels of her feet rose above the lawn's vegetation. I watched her tiptoe, arms out like a bird. The grass was long. Neither my sister nor I could handle the scythe, and our shears were dull. The nearest neighbor, Mr. Clemins, had yet to come and care for our landscaping this week. He lived five miles down the way, and it had occurred to me that he may be taking advantage of our circumstances. The details of our predicament. Sister called it an "ailment." I preferred the term "predicament." He was paid handsomely by our Aunt Helen, who looked over the estate's financials.

Gora floated in long slow steps. Her arms rocked up and down like Barbette, the great trapeze artist. Her nightgown caressed her ankles as her hair swayed back and forth over her shoulders. The yard's edge lay a few feet away, and my anxiety began to climb, causing me to clench my teeth.

Father would slap my hand when he caught me doing as such. "A trip to the dentist is not something you want to endure, Daughter. Please, please set your mind to depress your tensions."

I relaxed my jaw as she took the final steps. Gora looked back with a wicked smile as she stepped not one foot but two across the border. She spun and clapped her hands together. I let out a shriek, and the excitement made my heart flutter. A buzz, much like the hummingbird's invisible wings, filled my ears.

I cupped my hands to my mouth and chirped. "Come back, Sister, before they get you!"

Although I was sure I couldn't see her eyes from this distance, they rolled as she stepped back onto our property. She froze, and her face went sullen. I was unaware that my sister had become dispatched.

June 5th Diary Entry

After our evening tea, Gora began the events that would take her from me physically. We ate a modest dinner and exchanged gifts. She enjoyed hers, licking her lips and fingers as she devoured the pastries. I showed her the attack on my legs, and she nodded, sticking her forefinger and thumb together and watching a small string of honey stretch between them.

Her gift was a beautiful card made from birch bark—a painted scene depicting us enjoying a picnic in our backyard, surrounded by trillium and blue flag. It was beautiful, and I expressed it as much. She just nodded with a curt smile. I remember asking her if she were ill, and I cannot recall her verbal response. But I keep forever the actions that unfolded. She stood and put her sticky thumb in her mouth.

All of this felt like a dream. I am trying to relate the emotions that embodied me, but I have trouble placing them accurately. What was I feeling besides fear, Sister? I think I may never be able to recall it. Everything swam in horror. Your eyes, Sister. When I investigated their ocean, they were void of you. You left me to sit in that room in silence. I had no mind to know that you went into the kitchen to be with Mother.

Not as I, capturing what once was through reminiscing. Truly be with Mother. To leave me alone, here. I entered the kitchen out of the inability to be among my thoughts. You stood near the sink holding a box of Red Squill. I knew very little of the rodent repellant outside the history of its origin. *Drimia maritima.* A species of flowering plant that, if mixed in high doses, will kill rodents. I remember that particular box, now empty in your hand, was more than half full. Your lips, covered in the powder, opened and closed. Your eyes flared in fear.

You swallowed, your throat expanding as you gagged. I began to panic. When you dropped the box and began to scream, I covered my ears and trembled, and I do not know why. I watched liquid shoot from your mouth, expelling my pastries at your feet. I closed my eyes until I heard your weight collapse to the floor. I am ashamed to admit I held that position for the latter part of an hour.

My memory of the account, concerning my awakening to find you dead the following day, is jaded. It is the belief that my grief has caused the details to be convoluted. You had somehow made it to your bed, and there was only me, so it must be assumed I had, somehow, unbelievably so, carried you. When I woke, your corpse was warm, and I had taken you to be asleep. It was not until I placed my cheek near your lips that I realized you had abandoned me.

June 6th Diary Entry

It has been several hours, and I could not return to you. My imagination, if indeed it were, painted you in a rotten state. Flesh drooping from the bone, your now opaque orbs, milky with death, behind dark eyelids. Could you hear me, floating around the mansion like an otherworldly spy? Yes, Sister, I have sinned, as you know. I firmly believe you are here because you cannot bear to be without me and not because you wish to tattle to our maker. I am torn with jealousy with your current state, and yet the confusion of it haunts me. Floating through the walls, learning its depths of secrets, the knowledge of it. But you left me. You chose to test the heel biters and paid the highest price. Are they there with you? Do you see them? Their inability to hide from your gaze within shadows or corners of sight? What do they look like, Sister? Do they have ferocious teeth? They must. My scars are white grooves, raising mountains upon my flesh—a reminder of their veracity.

I often run my fingertips up and down my arms and legs. I read the demonic braille, my eyes darting to and fro, pantomiming their incantations. My hair stiffens at the very thought of it all. I sit in our living room. I say "our" because, for me, you will never truly be gone, even if the doctors diagnose me with mind sickness. They would be wrong, even if they were British. I drink my tea and wonder what I should do with you.

I cannot remove you. I haven't the constitution. Besides, where would I put you? Outside? No! What was I thinking? The rudeness in such thoughts demands that I straighten my nerves before thinking further. How I wish Father were here. Although entirely within my imagination, I smell his pipe, closing my eyes and letting it comfort me. I am tired. I think I shall nap on the loveseat. Please watch over me, Sister. Keep the heel biters at bay and awaken me upon the fifth hour.

June 6th Diary Entry

Sitting up blind in the darkness of the living room, I placed my hand across my heart and felt it patting against my palm. Remembering your physical absence, the depths of the space became cryptic. I could not sense you then, and I feared you had gone wherever it was souls go. To the maker, perhaps. I paced the halls in my dreams, trying to find Mother's song. Upon awakening, I felt the joy of escaping it, but now, now, I sit in the silence of fear. I look above, knowing your corpse lay with its milky eyes watching for my return. I put my bare feet on the cold wood of the floor and felt death creep up my ankles. As I approached the window, the brightness of the morning stung me. It was a surreal landscape, the yard's edges disappearing like a cruel magician. The bees and hummingbirds dance among the flower beds, ignorant of your evils. I question their validity.

When I entered the kitchen to make tea, the box of Red Squill lay on the floor, its remnants dusting a trail to where you collapsed. That is when I heard the rattle. I turned my head, although my nerves warned me not to. The sound was familiar, and I followed its call. Sister, I will not spread false rumors when I say my mind may not be sane. I fear I may have lost control over its sensibilities.

The door to Father's library shook on its hinges, and the sweet smell of Father's pipe emitted from behind. I wanted to call his name, but fear engulfed me again, and I stood like a statue waiting for death to take me. My heart raced as my jaw went slack. The door opened slowly, and mangled fingers slid out like branches, gripping the metal casing of its knob. I reached my hand out, protesting its advance, unable to scream, my heart hammering in my chest. A coldness crawled up my backside, caressing my lower back and hugging my form.

I heard from you then, Sister. A soft coo that made me moan with pleasure. "Down came the rain and washed the spider out."

When I awoke on the floor, the moon had cast a beam through the living room window, splitting the void. Has it been merely a day? I cannot recall. My stomach ached with hunger, and I rubbed it to quiet its cries. My legs were loose, and I hobbled to the loveseat, sitting in the room's darkness. I did not know it then, but I was traveling down the path that would bring you to me. I shivered, goosebumps cascading over my pale arms. The moonlight made me look deathly. You are colder than I, and I cannot believe I could dwell with you in that state. I rose on shaky limbs and made small quiet steps to the staircase. I needed to see you. I needed to know. Sister, I swear on the graves of our heritage that when I saw you sitting at the foot of the bed, my heart leaped with joy as my mind froze in fear.

(Loose page found within the Diary)

I stood at the door and watched your silhouette perched on the bed like a sentinel. What were you watching for? Me, perhaps? Rivulets of breath circled your crown like a wreath. Breath? It cannot be. All of this is madness. The British doctors in Father's tomes spoke of mind illness and hereditary sickness. Was it not our late Uncle Robert, who went mad with fever, killing his neighbor? It was, and our family forbade its retelling. The exact details made my tongue acrid with bile. Have I been cursed with his blood? Was it I who caused your demise, Sister? I surely did not give you the sense to eat the poison. The room was too silent. If a mouse had placed footing, I would assure you of its path. I hurried away. I could not see you in this state any longer, Sister. Sounds from within the walls echoed, and I wondered if it were Mother. I fled to the foot of the stairs and covered my ears, squeezing my head, the smell of father's acrid pipe filling my nostrils.

Down came the rain.

I spun to see you hovering at the top of the stairs. My mind began to reel as your figure loomed over me like a ghastly thing. I swear on our secrets, Sister, that you smiled at me just then. I could see the whites of your eyes as they danced beneath the shadows of your floating hair. Are they with you? The heel biters. I must be falling into the family curse, for I felt them nipping at my heels, Sister. I turned and ran for the door, flinging it open. The sun stabbed at me, and I shielded my eyes.

Not looking back nor waiting for your descent, I ran down the concrete steps into the vastness of the yard.

Down came the rain.

I dare not look back at you. I could feel you on my heels. It was them. The biters were with you. The blades slashed at my naked calves when my feet swept through the grass. I focused. I had no other way, Sister, to be with you. To be with Father. To be with Mother. The yard stretched out as if warning me, telling me to return to the house's safety. I could not.

I extended my hands, reaching for the yard's edge, pleading with time. I paused at the border and turned. The shadow of you slithered across the yard like a great serpent, a black mist breathing, killing the vegetation. I raised my hand to my mouth to shield it from your foul-smelling essence. My eyes widened as you approached me, your mouth gaping as if ready to devour me. It is not you, Sister. It is them. I know this as truth. I closed my eyes and stepped over the border as you caressed my form.

We washed the spider out.

I Died Saturday

The line of cars leads back to the main road like it always has. This coffee shop has some of the best latte choices in town, not to mention the bagels. Although the Roast Cafe is a very bland name, it is all the rave here in little Durnam, Ohio. Northeast Ohio small towns are not the treasure chest of tourism, especially Durnam. It has several nicknames, none of which I laugh about anymore now that I am stuck here. When I graduated from high school, my dreams were more significant. My hopes were also large, and both hit the wall of reality that same summer.

I was only nineteen, and my income, or lack thereof, put me with the majority of this town's population of eighteen thousand. Poverty is a word I try never to use. I choose phrases like "missed opportunities" and "small-town environment" to explain why I am less fortunate. The elderly like to use fancy titles for their failing city. I once overheard a man explaining it to a tourist. I could tell by the visitor's intrigued expression that he was amusing him at best, calling this town "the center of the Durnam Micropolitan Statistical Area."

What the fuck did that even mean?

As always, I rolled my eyes and closed my brain to the conversation.

The line moves up a few cars, and we slide into the parking lot and out of the busy road. I get quite a bit more comfortable. Sitting in the middle of the road is dangerous, and I look at myself in the side mirror. I fix my hair. The golden locks, previously dyed bright green, look over-bleached. My makeup is subtle, and my eyes are bloodshot from last night's three-hour nap. I notice a stain on my t-shirt, and I recline back in the seat and exhale a little louder than necessary. My boyfriend looks at me from the driver's side and smiles.

"Alyssa, babe." he squints his eyes. "You moody this morning? Again?"

I tilt my head down and peer at him from under my eyebrows. Faking my annoyance, I reach over and pinch his underarm. He recoils with a yelp, and we both chuckle. I turn and look out the window at the passing cars. Kevin was not my first choice for a boyfriend, and my parents showed the same wonderment. He was from an impoverished family, worse off than mine, and, to be honest, the town looked down on them. They were in constant trouble with the law. His brother,

Jeremy, older by ten years, served more than a year in prison. I never knew what for, and Kevin never wanted to discuss it. The word around town is that it involved a minor and some pretty lewd activity. I also heard he robbed a gas station and had a real gun. I always hoped for the second story.

We started our relationship with an argument. He was loud-mouthed, and I got tired of hearing it. Several months of "Shut the fuck up, Kevin," and "Why don't you shut up, slut." drew us closer until one day, my friend Jeff said, "Why don't you two just bang and get it over with?"

After three parties that summer, we found ourselves hanging out away from the others. The last party resulted in this. Us. We. I don't know what it is, but it is.

We finally roll up to the drive-through. Kevin rolls down his window as a bitchy, high-pitched voice comes over the speaker.

"Good morning. What can I get for you."

Kevin looks over at me, and I roll my eyes and look back out the window. The voice belongs to Karen Strakle. Voted most likely to be president of the United States but was, in actuality, The Roast's manager. I almost feel worse for her than myself—all that expectation to wind up stuck here, like me. Kevin orders a regular coffee, three creams, and one sugar. I get an iced mocha with extra whipped cream. We resume our drive to work. Kevin works at Drifty's car parts store, and now I have an office job. I reach over and hold his hand. I am not looking at him, but I can feel him look over and smile. He loves me. I guess I love him. I don't know. All I do know is I do not want to work today… well, any day.

My office floor is number 6. I moved to the design team after my wall design fiasco in the main showroom. This small-time clothing boutique is the talk of the town. It caters to the goth crowd, which I never knew was still a thing. People say I have a "goth style." Sporting black shirts, sporting cryptic messages like, "People are gross" or "Save the animals from ourselves," matched with tight black skinny jeans or a skirt, also black.

I don't know.

I thought my style was me. I never looked for a label and didn't need to be in a crowd or a clique. But, to the suits upstairs, I am what embodies their vision.

Which is what? Dark? I don't know.

One day, I walked through the showroom to get a coffee and saw this ridiculous display. It is the most extensive wall in the store. A huge mosaic of rock band posters mixed with clothing from their most popular collections. The first thing you see when entering the main floor. It looked cluttered, stupid, and a corporate sellout all at the same time. Go figure.

When I mentioned this, the manager smirked and said, "If you think you can do better, Miss Alyssa," she turns, looking at the mess, "have at it." She looked back with a sarcastic grin on her face and stared. "I hope you get fired." She snapped her fingers and walked into the back room.

She always uses "Miss" in front of every female's name. It is annoying, but she thinks it is demeaning. She scoffs at the male employees, flicks her tongue between her teeth, makes a sucking sound before walking away. She is a bitch.

I went to the storeroom closet and found a ladder. It took only a few hours to arrange the mural of T-shirts and posters by year. Color-coordinating it to look like street art. When the manager returned, she smiled, "Fired for sure," and walked around the showroom, laughing with other managers.

The next day, they called me into the office. Then, they relocated me upstairs to design their billboards and ads. Making the store's interior in what the suits called "Alyssa's vision." I thought it was stupid. I was ready to laugh and return to my sales job until the raise and cool office made me stuff my opinions in the trash. I need security. Now, the managers get me coffee as I ridicule their work. It is worth it for now.

I enter my office and walk to the small window overlooking the main street. The people below look like tiny insects. Some are walking with smaller insects and having conversations. I wouldn't be caught dead participating in their overexpressed laughs and fake sentiments. I walk away and enter a small bathroom. Sitting on the toilet, I look at Instagram for an infinite time until I hear a knock at the door.

Suits.

I put my phone on the sink next to me and clean up. I stand and face the mirror.

Blonde.

I liked my green better, but part of the offer came with the hair change. The suits like my clothing as it came from their line, but the hair had to go. Not corporate savvy when business comes to visit.

"You have to look professional as well, Alyssa." My boss educated me.

Bullshit. You only have to talk about money and make cool designs. These people do not give a shit about what I look like, Ken.

They showed me the money and, to prove my point earlier, I am now blonde. It is always about money.

Ken peeks in before I even get a chance to exit the bathroom. "Alyssa?"

His tone carries like he didn't know I was in there. He gave me his "We got business later" look when I got off the elevator this morning. I slip my phone into my pocket, walk to my desk, and plop into the chair. Ken walks over and stands at the head of my desk, smiling down at me like some mad hatter. He is a mousy man: six foot, thirty-five years old, and no more than one hundred and forty-five pounds. He always wears dark blue suits with an ugly, bright tie. Usually, purple. I don't see how he thinks they match. His shirts are always some variants of his tie choice. Hair pressed to his head, his face looks like he is always squinting. Ken was a numbers man and came from some big university in Boston.

"What's up today, Ken?" I say with my right hand, shading my eyes as if I have a headache.

I do, but I am dramatic. He tilts his smile to a frown,

"There is a man to see you downstairs, and he looks…" he pauses, and I wait.

He doesn't continue. I look up at him, letting my hand drop. It slaps against the armrest of my seven-hundred-dollar office chair. He looks away as if scanning the room for something, then looks back at me with a pissed expression.

"Well," he takes a breath, closing his eyes, and then widens them in a severe glare, "we will say 'disheveled.'"

I push my face out and squint my eyes at him as if this excessive expression will change what he has said or make him go away. Ken stares at me until I throw my hands up, more dramatic acting. I slide my chair back and stand with an exhale that exaggerates the effort, and I walk out of the office with him.

Ken takes quick steps beside me and stares ahead. "I hope he is not a relative of yours?"

I don't know if I should be insulted or not. We enter the elevator, and I push the ground floor button. Ken is a dick sometimes.

Elevator rides are awkward. People pack in and face forward, pretending no one else is there. Someone will look over and smile out of politeness. No one knows if that is a genuine sentiment. When only two people are in an elevator, it is a moment of silence, even if you work together. Realizing that you don't want to be in close quarters. I look straight ahead but can feel Ken look over with his little mousy eyes.

Finally, the door opens to the main showroom floor. He holds his arm out and bows his head, again, another preconceived polite sentiment. I exit and look around the room. Everyone is talking to customers while working. The store is bustling and alive. *I miss it.* I never thought I would hear those words from my inner voice, but I miss it. Ken walks past me and looks up at me, his head tilted down, looking from under his eyebrows. I take a deep breath and follow. We pass a few teens looking at plastic jackets with chains and spray paint designs. They slip them on, look at each other, and giggle. Good luck getting mommy and daddy to buy that for you at three hundred dollars.

We pass a few employees chatting, and Ken puts his hand to his mouth and pretends to clear his throat. They look up, and he gives them a disapproving glare. They scatter, find the nearest customer, and never look back as we pass. I searched the crowd for this stranger. A tall, slender, odd-looking man stands by a fire exit on the east side of the building. He is wearing ill-fitting baggy jeans and an off-white button-up shirt. His hair, combed but disheveled in appearance, is a peppered brown. He looks like an average guy from an average town. Looks like he is from… well, here. His hands slumped in his pockets, and he scanned the room with big, wide brown eyes.

The stranger's stare looks manic but calm if that makes any sense. I don't think it does, to be honest. I look down, and the man is wearing old shoes. Not old as in fashion or worn from the trials of everyday life. I mean, old. Like they are from the nineteen twenties. It didn't make sense. They were black wingtips, polished with clean tied laces. But you couldn't afford a nice pair of jeans and a button-up? I have seen weirder things and shake off the notion as I approach him. He turns his head and looks straight at me. His face brightens, and he grins a vast, white-toothed smile. It makes me reconsider the calm but manic assumption. Let's go with manic. His eyes are more expansive, and the brown resembles a caramel and chocolate swirl. I can't help but stare as I extend my hand.

"Hello, I am..."

"Alyssa Stockton!" he interrupts, pulling his right hand from his pocket and with a firm but gentle grip shakes mine.

His voice sounds excited. Like we are long-lost relatives or best friends from high school, but I do not know this man. I pull my gaze from his eyes and take in his face. Now, I can see he has soft, perfect skin, not a wrinkle. His skin radiates a glow that makes me reconsider his clothes. He may be one of those eccentric types. Millions of dollars and houses in the Hamptons. High-end sports cars, and resort passes year-round, but fuck clothes, right? You see these people on television all the time. Johnny Depp is like this. Wearing old boots with duct tape around the toes. He rolls cigarettes while purchasing five-hundred-dollar bottles of wine. They get popped open and never drunk. Well, that's what the magazines and shows say anyway.

When he pulls his hand away, he seems taller. He has an erect stature that looms and makes me feel uncomfortable.

"Do I know you?" I ask, my voice a little shaky.

Ken looks at me, puzzled, and then back at the stranger. My throat feels tight and dry. The man slips his hand back into his pocket and wobbles on his heels like a ten-year-old boy, smiling and staring.

"So, you do not remember me?" He looks puzzled, smiling like a fool.

I shake my head and look at Ken, who looks more confused than me. The stranger pulls a card from his left-hand pocket and extends it to me.

"My name is William Cortis."

He pauses when I take the card, then slips his hand back into his pocket. He wobbles again with that smile stretched across his face. He leans in.

"You were only six years old when we met, but I was sure my face would have left an impression."

I look away, thinking.

"I would say so, yes," I answer. "But I don't remember you, so what's this about."

He leans back, and his smile fades. He spins and begins to walk toward the exit. I look at Ken, and we share bewilderment before looking back at the man.

"Call the number on the card," the stranger calls, holding up one hand and extending two fingers in a peace sign. "I have a package for you that needs delivering," he continues. "Most important."

He raises his voice as he slides the hand back into his pocket and walks out the door to the street. I want to chase after him, but I am so confused at what happened that I am frozen. Ken stares at me and shakes his head in awe. Turning, he finds some employees chatting, rushes toward them, and begins to harass them. I look down at the card and return to the elevator.

When I shut my office door, the room feels empty and spacious. My mind is reeling with questions, and I am hyper-fixated on the stranger. Why would I not remember a face like that? Is he some whack job off the street? A fan of my work? I shake my head. An obsessed fan?

Ok, Alyssa, like you have fans. You make ads and display pieces, dumbass. You're not Nate Burkus.

I walk across the room and study the card again. The paper is bone white with beautiful ornate carvings. The edges are sharp and coated. The typeface is bold, dark black. I toss the card on the desk and plop down in my chair. Then, I see it. The surface of the card shines from the angle on which I am sitting and, behind the text, embedded in the card stock, is a symbol. A circle with lines running through in all directions. When I sit up and look down at the card, they disappear. Only when I pick it up and tilt it do they reappear. I place the card back down on my desk and push the page button on my phone. A beep blast interrupts the silence of the room.

"Yes?" The receptionist answers, sounding annoyed.

I stare at the card. "Can you send James from graphic design to my office immediately?"

There is a brief pause, and then she responds, less annoyed. "Right away, Miss Stockton."

I lean back as the phone beeps, and silence fills the room. "Who the fuck is William Cortis?"

Ken peeks his head in, looking hard at me. Weird that I know he expects me to be slouching at my desk. Does that say more about him or me? He opens the door a little wider and squeezes through as if it can only open inches. The graphic designer pushes the door open and strolls in behind Ken. He looks around the office space and then at me. Ken smiles and backs out the door without a further glance or word.

"Wow!" His smile shows his cheap veneers. "I have yet to be in one of these offices."

He walks over and stands in front of my desk, hands in his pockets. He wears faded khakis, a button-up white shirt, and a cloth tie to make his cheap teeth look less affordable. His hair is light blonde, wavy, and shoulder-length. I can smell what must be hand-me-down cologne from his older brother or dad. I'll bet he got it for Christmas from his mom. I am not sure of his age, but he could be no more than twenty-four or twenty-six. I lean up, grab the card from my desk, and toss it to the edge before him. It almost slides off when he pulls his right hand from his pocket and snatches it up, looking at it uninterested. He looks over the top of it at me and smiles again. I want to punch him.

"A gentleman dropped that off to me, and I wondered if you could do me a favor."

He looks back at the card and makes a more attractive look.

"If you tilt the card a little," I tilt my head, as an example, and he follows suit, holding it up above his brow line, "you can see a weird logo that looks…" I pause for a second, thinking of the correct terminology.

"Oh, it is embossed, it looks like." he interrupts, looking back down at me. He looks back at the card and puzzles over the shape. He turns it back and forth in the light, trying to make out what it is, and shrugs after a few attempts.

"Want me to take it back with me and figure out what that design is, don't ya?"

I nod in agreement, and he looks back at it.

"Should be quick," he says, then palms the card, sliding it into his pocket, and looks up at me, smiling.

"I'll send it back with what I find. Give me a few days."

He leaves my office without asking if I need the card back.

Asshole.

I sit, processing the situation that has unfolded, when my desk phone buzzes. I push the intercom, and the secretary's voice chimes in.

"Mr. Flander will send an email with a picture of the card if you need its information as he processes your request."

Is this guy psychic?

"Thank you," I respond and lean back in my chair.

Still an asshole.

I slide open my file cabinet to my right and pull out my laptop.

Who the fuck is William Cortis?

I open the computer, listen to the hum as it comes alive, and lean back in my chair again. I watch the screen flicker, reveal the home screen, and sit up to enter my password. I am thinking about the card. The way he was so smug as he walked out into the street.

Remember me? What the fuck!

A picture of Curt Cobain pops up, and I immediately mouse over the internet icon and double-click. The browser opens, and I type "William Cortis" and hit enter. Nothing. I scroll down. Nothing of relevance includes those names together. I got many Williams, and I even got Billy Cortis. A fifteen-year-old kid from Englewood, Florida. A Boy Scout troop. Him with a beach cleanup in 2002.

I sit back and bite at one of my thumbnails, a habit I started in the fifth grade when Mr. Jennis asked me to sing a solo at a choir recital. I could never seem to break it. It is my go-to when I get nervous or have anxiety.

Why am I nervous?

I need a coffee. Slamming the lid on the laptop, I get up, walk to the elevator, and push the button. Ken comes around the corner, sees me, and begins to pick up the pace. I slide into the elevator and push the close button in rapid succession. I can hear Ken approach.

"Really, Alyssa!"

I start to laugh as I press the button for the lobby and move to the back. When the entrance opens, I peer out and look both ways.

Ken took the stairs, but he couldn't be that quick.

Sixth floor. What are you? Superman, Ken? I approach the front door and step out into the sun.

I turn left and head down the sidewalk, disappearing into the crowd. It isn't my lunch break, but I need breathing room for inspiration. These suits don't care what I do. It is always about the result. I make my way down a few blocks and then hail a cab. I slide in.

"Any coffee shop more than five miles from here, please."

The man pulls into traffic, and I sit back, panting. Pulling my phone from my pocket, I flip through my contacts, find the number, and dial. No one answers.

My work can be challenging to explain for reasons beyond comprehension, but it is as simple as the laws of the land. The work is necessary. I cannot exist with multitudes of like-minded individuals proclaiming my throne. The air is stiff as the sun beats down between the trees. Its rays look like arrows in the natural beauty of the forest. The silence is deafening. My ears ring, longing for the recent sounds of the city to which I have grown accustomed. The mindless chatter of strangers with their little lives that they deem necessary, the small details of everyday existence and the hum of human frailties. Quite sad.

The boy lies there, dirt draping his body, making the earthy bed seem welcoming. I want to lie down next to him and rest. How can a small child understand that this is necessary? I saved him, and I was sure he would never quite know or understand how. Children have a sense of innocence that I must avoid when doing my work. He was eight years old and lived on Pressler Street. That was all I knew. It was all I needed to know, given the circumstances. His chest cavity is open to the sun and resembles a tiny birdcage. Its ribs curl out. He would feed animals in the coming days and make a lovely home for small rodents and worms. The cycle would be pleased with this gift. My work, although not my creation, is necessary work. There cannot be more than one of us here. It is a too-small world for a collective like us. His face points toward the treetops. Arms spread out and palms facing up. I like this pose. I understand that the law enforcement officers will tie a label to this. "Serial." That is fine. In a way, it is nice to put a human title to what I am doing.

The sun spreads over his face, and his open eyes stare wide-eyed. It is beautiful. He had such a short run in this existence, but there would be other opportunities for him. I positioned the boy's legs so they would be completely engulfed in the earth. Soil covers part of his pelvis. He is too young to have his dignity exposed to the human eye. The staring of law enforcement officers and the person who will come across his remains. Like most of my work, I want their bodies found after months of environmental exposure. It is less hardening on the mind, especially with youth. The features are less recognizable.

I breathe in, closing my eyes to let the sun turn the blackness behind my eyelids to hues of orange and yellow. The warmth covers my face in a blanket of serene divinity. A peacefulness in this vast forest that I alone enjoy in its silence. I look down and place my hands in my pockets. It is time to go. I take one last glance before making my way down the hill into the depths of the wood, soon to see the hikers and civilization rearing its mundane head. As I walk, I listen to the snapping of tree limbs beneath my feet. Like the snapping of weak bones. Nature is murder. The smell of rotten wood and soft pine fills my senses and confuses my mind with the reality of death, and its counterpart. Little scurries in pine needles to my right. Creatures going about their lives unthreatened by my intrusion. Birds above rustle in the trees and stare down at me in silence as I approach their nests.

Nature is foolish, vicious, beautiful, and intelligent. I understand why people often want to be in its glory. Escaping their steel fortresses and deadlines. Resting their minds on more subtle things. Most of them are unaware that it was more dangerous out here than in their manufactured palaces. Much more.

I come to a clearing, stop in my tracks, and bend down, my head swimming with a ping.

Already?

I finished my work on the boy today, and already another. My brain shot pins of light through the backs of my eyes. A faint voice echoed like a cooing mother talking to her newborn child.

"Alyssa." The name faded into my mind's eye. "The daughter of the sinful."

I stand and rub my temples, opening my eyes wide to refocus. I take deep breaths and peer at the sky, the pine trees swaying in rhythm with nature's breath.

"Alyssa," I say to the treetops. "The daughter of the sinful?"

I close my eyes and nod my head in acceptance of the contract. The pact. My work. I continue my descent to the main trail and back to where the people live. I will wait for another sign—more information.

"Alyssa," my mind repeats as I walk down the path.

Every step vibrates up my spine from the hard dirt road, each vibration in time with her name. There is no place for more than one, and I am coming for you.

I wouldn't say I like booth seats. Especially when they try to update them to make you feel the trend is still acceptable. People under the age of forty-five do not seem to like booth seating. My opinion.

"I would say that was an assumption with little or no research."

I look to the left of the doorway. William Cortis sits in a booth beside a large plate glass window with a frosted coffee logo. His attire is different now. He has on an old Iron Maiden T-shirt and a ballcap that rests on sandy blonde hair. His eyes are an ashen gray. I would never have known it was him if he hadn't spoken. My mind is racing. He stares at me, elbows on the table. Leaning back, he makes a gesture for me to sit. I hesitate. He nods, looking down at the empty booth seat across from him, and then stares at me like he is about to pierce my soul. He is.

"I think you underestimate the power and comfort of the booth, Alyssa." He pauses and smiles, his teeth pristine white, perfect, and straight. "Try it out," he gestures and looks down at the seat. I circle the back of the booth seat, scanning the room. People are chatting. Some play chess or are reading books. They are most definitely not concerned about the creepy guy asking the young lady to sit in the booth. I slide into the seat, and as I look up, a woman approaches and places a hot medium cup of black coffee in front of me. She looks down and smiles, looking uncomfortable. Her eyes are glassy and distant. Both hands shake as she places the cup before me. She retracts them in what seems like slow motion. The woman smiles and wipes only her fingertips on her coffee-stained apron.

"Enjoy, Alyssa. It's on the house."

My skin becomes clammy, and the hair on my neck prickles, warning me that I need to get the fuck out.

William leans back and looks around the room. "This is quite the place, Alyssa. Do you come here often?"

He lets out a single chuckle before I could completely open my mouth.

"No."

He takes a breath. "This isn't your style." He pauses, puts both hands on the table, and drums his fingers. "The booths, right?"

I look down at my coffee, my whole body trembling. My chest feels heavy. I am going to die.

How did this guy find me? How did he even know I was coming here? What the hell is going on?

My anxiety begins to turn to anger, and I look up at him, my ears and cheeks burning.

"What is all this about?"

He sits in silence.

"You don't know my family, and I don't know you." I pause and take a deep breath, holding it until my lips quiver. Letting out a long, slow breath, I continue. "You hand me some bullshit story and card, and then poof, you're gone."

He widens his eyes a little and lets me continue uninterrupted.

"I leave…"

"Ran away," he interjects.

I pause a moment.

"Escape," I continue, "to find you here," I look around the coffee shop, "a random place I tell a cab driver to pick. With a waitress…"

"Barista," he interrupts.

I stare at him, and my ears begin to get hot.

This guy is an asshole.

"To get free coffee, on the house, by name, and I have never, *never*…" I raise my voice and a few people stop to acknowledge my outburst, then returned to their activities, "*never*," I continue, lowering my shaky voice, "been to this shop."

He raises his right hand and snaps his fingers. The sound is so crisp, so loud that I jump. I squint from the high-pitched crack, and the sound distorts, pushing my eardrums back. Wincing, I manage not to cover my ears in defense. When I look up, the room had become dead. Is that the right word? Yes. Some people sit frozen in mid-laugh, reaching for chess pieces, turning pages, workers pouring coffee, the liquid frozen in mid-pour, the steam hovering just above their containers. The ringing in my ears begins to fade, and silence fills the space. William sits across from me and lowers his hand.

I am confused. *What is happening?*

He places both hands on the table and looks around the room. "I think we need to start over, Alyssa."

He concentrates his eyes on me, and they seem to become fluid, like gas. The gray turns black and then back to gray, like cloudy water. My heart begins to race. My hands rest on the tabletop, my fingers feeling like pins. I can feel him caress the top of my hand, and I want to pull away. His contact slows my heart rate, and I feel a calm overtake me. He smiles and removes his hand, sitting back in his seat. I can hear the plastic fabric crinkle, moving the space around us. Every breath I take is in perfect synch with his. Each sound emanates from his movement.

"Now, listen to me," he says in a smooth, low tone.

I am hypnotized by its vibration.

"I am here for one purpose: to save myself."

His voice echoes a delay that fills my head. Each syllable is fading into the next, and I want to cry.

"He will come for you because he wants me. I am within you and have been since you accepted me."

A tear runs down my cheek, and the heat warms my skin.

"I do know your father. I entered him when he was a younger man," he pauses, the delay repeating the word "younger," fading into the back of my mind. More tears.

He smiles. "Your father had made many mistakes, Alyssa, but none so grave as the one that day in the woods."

His breathing steadies my mind, my tears slow.

"When he allowed himself to murder those children, he allowed us in. He is not the only one." His eyes narrowed. "Your father is of no consequence now. He will be gone."

I take a breath, and my chest shakes. *Gone? What does he mean gone?*

"Gone," he answers. "He will come for him. There is no reason to worry. No one will cry for his soul, Alyssa." His smile stretches across his face like a crazed clown. "You have more things to worry about than your father's secrets, his sickness."

He reaches across the table and runs his fingertips across my forearm. I calm.

"He is coming for you once he learns that I left your father. He doesn't want us all here." He removes his hand from mine. "He wants to be the only one."

His breathing becomes slow and ragged. His eyes calm, and he begins to look sad. His eyes weep with emotion, although no tears form in their sockets.

"He will kill you like he will your father. He knows now." He smiles. "He knows your name and is coming for the sinner's daughter." He leans in. "You will never see me again, Alyssa, but I am in your mind. I am part of you. We are one. If you die, I go back to the void."

His eyes become serious. Darker. Filling with a blackness that seemed endless. "You, however…"

He pauses. The noise of the room fills me, and I now feel alone. I look up. My eyes well with hot tears, and I wipe my arm across my eyes.

"You ok, Hun?"

I look over to see the barista standing at the end of my table. William is gone. My head swims, and I feel myself nod.

"You need a refill?"

She places her hand on my shoulder. I flinch a little, and she pulls away and gives me a shocked look. She walks toward the next booth. Everyone seems unaware of the passing events. My heart pounds in my chest like a hammer, as my mind matches its pace. I look at the empty seat in front of me. I can still feel William's presence. His voice echoes in my mind.

We are one.

What was his real name? What was all this insanity about my dad? Children?

I tried to reach back into my memories. I was trying to catch a moment.

What did my dad do? What is happening?

I looked down at my coffee and try to steady my mind. I reach for my cell in my pocket, open the contacts, look for my father's number, and hesitate. Wiping the remaining tears from my eyes, I push the dial. The phone rings a few times, each ring a ping that shakes my brain, rumbling my eardrums and making my head pound. I pull the phone away from my ear a little and wait. The ringing is interrupted.

"Hey, Kiddo!"

I take short breaths and steady my voice.

"Hi, Dad." My heart slows.

There was a slight pause. I broke the silence first. "Can we meet up? I need to talk to you."

Slight pause.

"Now, Kiddo?" I could hear his unsure breathing. "How about tomorrow?"

I look down at my coffee cup, clearing my throat to stop my voice from shaking.

He continues "I'll call you tonight. I have a visitor. I have to go. Ok, Kiddo?"

"A visitor?"

"Talk to you soon." He hangs up.

My hand begins to shake as a voice fills my mind. William.

He is there to take him. He will be gone.

I am pacing the street corner while waiting for the cab, and people give me looks and take wide steps away.

Look at the crazy girl. She's most likely on drugs.

The pavement begins to feel sticky on my feet. I look at my shoes to pretend I'm not the topic of ridicule. I can feel William in my spine, my brain, everywhere. Somehow, I am not sure how, I can feel him in my blood. He is pulsing within the rhythm of me.

Was he even he? It? Fuck!

The cab slams to a stop as close to the curb as possible before hopping it. I jump back as the driver, in a frantic motion, rolls down his window to a one-inch gap at eye level.

"Where to?" he yells in an Asian accent.

I look up. He tilts his head down, impatient with my awkward stare. I hurry to the back door and climb in.

"5th and Conrad," I say.

He looks in the rearview and pulls into traffic without a single mirror check.

"Please," I continue.

He is a middle-aged man with neat and tight black hair, trimmed around the ears. His eyes are almost a shiny black, and his skin has lines defining his mouth. He seems determined to kill us when he looks back. Putting two fingers in a peace sign, he looks in the rearview mirror and smiles.

"How is your day?" he says, a cheerful attitude quite different from when he first pulled up.

I look down at my hands and then out at the road. Cars seem to be driving in slow motion as we fly by them. I look back up at him, staring at me.

"I am fine," I say, raising my voice a little. "Could you please watch the road?"

He makes a small laugh as if I wouldn't hear him, and he looks back toward the front. I try to sit back and relax as I stare at the back of his seat.

Maybe the man at my father's house is a business associate.

It's not, a voice echoes somewhere in my consciousness.

Shut the fuck up! I say to myself.

I look up to see the driver looking back, making a concerned face. When he catches me staring back, he returns his attention to the road. I am sure I am not the first weirdo he's ever picked up, and I know I won't be the last.

The cab swerves in and out of traffic, and I brace myself, palming the seat on both sides of my hips.

If it is what William said...

It is, the voice interrupts.

I grit my teeth and shake my head. I can't believe that my father is some child killer. How could someone with an entire family hide that life?

Because he was good at it, the voice reasons.

I ignore him. *How did this thing find out he did these things? How did it enter? Possess?*

"Possess" is an easy term for you to understand, the voice says.

Shut up! I say in my thoughts.

Fine, it answers, *but you will need me in about five minutes.*

He can hear my thoughts! It makes sense if he is in me.

The hairs prickle on my neck again.

I seriously hope this is insanity.

It isn't, he says. *Or should I still shut up?*

I close my eyes tight.

I will get to my father's, or all of this will be for nothing. It was a client—everyday business. I will hug my father. Talk about my job, then leave. I will then immediately check myself into the nearest psychiatric ward. Hey, Dad, your daughter is fucking nuts!

I wish it were the case, he says, his voice echoing behind my eyes. *But it is not.*

I slap my head with my open palm. The driver looks back again, then at the road, continuing to the destination. We turn on 5th and head down the two blocks to Conrad. He pulls up to the curb, slams the car into park, and pulls a clipboard from the passenger seat.

"Twenty-five even," he smiles from the rearview.

I fumble in my pockets and pull out some cash. I unravel some money, find two twenty-dollar bills, and hand them over the seat. He reaches over his shoulder and takes them, looking at them.

"Keep the change," I say, getting out of the car before he can speak.

I walk around the back and cross the street. I look back to see the cab pull away with a screech, not bothering to look where I am going.

As the sun beats down on my face, I walk a block and begin feeling light-headed. The neighborhood is silent, not like in my youth. Kids on bikes used to hang out, passing around cigarettes they had stolen from their parents. Girls flirted with boys as the boys showed off for the girls. Now, the streets look like an Old West film. Not a soul anywhere. I come to my father's driveway. A big, black, cast-iron gate rises ten feet, making him look important compared to the neighbors. I stop and bend over as my head swims. I feel like I am going to vomit. After a few minutes, I shake it off and continue to the edge of the walkup.

A pole hangs out from a bush with a clear plastic cover. Lifting it, I push a red button. I look up, and the sun stabs my eyes. I put my hand up to shield them and look through the gate toward the front of the house. After a few minutes, I lift the plastic cover and push the button again, holding it a little longer.

He won't answer, Kiddo. He's dead.

I look back through the gate, and my heart begins to pound.

Long dead, the voice continues.

"Shut the fuck up, William," I mumble, and I back down the sidewalk and begin to walk into the next block.

The neighbor owns a tree that hangs over the lower section of my father's fence. It took three months of township meetings and civil court hearings. Dad finally gave up and let the neighbor keep his tree, stating, "Let him have the damn thing, it will eventually rot. Then, the prick will have to pay to remove it. I win."

Yet, here was the tree, standing tall and looking strong. I smile as I grab the gate and begin to use the tree as leverage as I scale the short section of fence. It seemed much more complicated and dangerous when I was young. I steady my balance and then hold my breath and jump, landing with a roll in the backyard.

Oh, the concerns and trials of the young, William says with a small laugh.

"If I kill myself, would you go back to the void?" I ask aloud.

There is a slight pause, and then he laughs.

Possibly, he chuckles, *if you have the balls to go through with it.*

I shake my head, annoyed, making my way across the yard in a low stance. I can't get as low as when I was a kid, my chest almost as low as my knees. I look back, ensuring my father doesn't appear at the doors or windows. Now, I look apish. Swinging my arms, bent over, my chest slumped. I come to the back of the house and stop near a bush about thirty feet from the back door. There is a large bay window to the left of the porch. I continue my ape crawl and stay eye-level to the bottom of the window.

The curtains, an ugly floral pattern resembling Victorian couches, block a clear vision of the living room.

Had he never changed them? How many years has it been?

Twenty-three years, William chimes in. *He bought them on a business trip to Cape Cod. It was your mother's birthday gift.*

I try to look through the flowers.

She was a needy bitch.

I pause and look at the ground. *Please...* I say to myself.

His echo stops, and he remains silent. I duck down and make my way down the wall toward the porch. Climbing onto the deck and then reaching the door, I grip the knob. It pops open with a snapping sound. I close my eyes and pause, taking a deep breath. I loosen my grip and pull the door open.

The entryway is dark and silent. I creep to the sidewall facing the living room. I picture my father and his guest sitting by the fireplace, talking about small business matters, and drinking his expensive brandy. No voices. No movement. I tilt my head to look in. Both chairs are facing the middle of the room.

My father is sitting in the chair closest to the kitchen entrance. His head is missing. Blood drapes his chest, his hands gripping the chair's armrests in a tight struggle. My chest heaves as I vomit onto the rug, my eyes watering, and my stomach lurching. I open my eyes as I purge, tears clouding my vision. I sit on the floor and begin to scream. My voice feels foreign.

I look up at my father. The air becomes thick. I struggle to catch my breath and calm myself.

Now that you have seen, we need to leave. He is here.

I ignore William. I try to steady myself as I tip over onto my side. I look away and back out toward the door to the backyard. I have to get out. I have to run. I roll onto my stomach, and the perfume of vomit fills my nose, making me dry heave. I crawl to the back door and push it open. The fresh air swims in and pulls the fragrance of my stomach bile from my nostrils. I take a deep breath and cough out hard, gagging. I begin to drag myself out to the porch when I hear his voice.

Alyssa.

The booming vocal rips up my spine and enters my brain like worms. Each syllable pulls at my senses, paralyzing me.

Your father, try as he may, could not keep you safe, could he?

I try to crawl, but my body stiffens, and a weight pushes down on my back, pinning me to the floor.

He never told you? the voice slurs.

I cannot answer. I close my eyes tight. William is gone. Like a snake, he slithered back into the recesses of my mind, hiding like a coward.

A snake, the man laughs. *He won't hide for long.*

Echoing laughter fills the room's corners.

I cannot tell if it is pure imagination or actual laughter.

He knows I am here for him, and he cannot escape me.

Every syllable claws at my skull, rakes my spine, and I cry out.

Do you know where you come from?

I feel my body relax, and the weight shifts from me. The pain fades, and I take a deep breath, cough, and roll over onto my back. The room is black shadows, and I can't see where he is.

Let me explain your position.

The voice comes from around the room as if he is everywhere, filling every inch of the darkness.

The door behind me slams shut, and a chair slides across the rug, stopping two feet to my right.

Sit and listen. You deserve that before you move on to the next realm.

I wipe my eyes with my sleeve and crawl over and up into the chair. I can feel the darkness engulf me, wrapping me in a hug. My breathing slows as I am lulled into a dream state. My eyes grow heavy. From behind the veil of my drooping eyelids, his voice slides down my spine and swims within my groin.

Let us start with your mother, the voice hisses.

Invisible hands massage my brain, echoing pulses like Morse code through my body. It feels as if my heart is slowing to a stop. I cannot tell if I am breathing anymore. My body goes limp, and I feel my essence lift from my prison.

Your father's first victim.

The room and its edges move further away, disappearing into a void, and I go with it.

Folk

It is better to drive at night. Everyone in Bret's family would argue against this technique, but he swore by it. He researched. Taking the measures necessary to ward off the dangers mentioned. He picked at his peas and kept his face low, adjusting his glasses every few seconds. They needed tightening, which he forgot to do before leaving. His insurance would threaten him about following through on his appointments.

"Sir, your co-pays are low enough that you can stay within the time frame to make appointments."

It was always a mousy-sounding lady who would ring his cell non-stop until he answered. He imagined she was an older lady, in her forties. She had tight, curly hair and sat straight at her more decorated table. She wore pressed shirts with flowers on them. Kakis, with no socks, and women's loafers. The do-gooder in the office. He adjusted his glasses and took a scoop of peas, balancing them on the fork as he slid it into his mouth. He couldn't give the lady a name but knew she would also have a picture of a canary on her desk. She couldn't have cats. She was too oppressive, nor could she have a dog because they were too overbearing. He would make the appointment when he returned from his trip next week. He swallowed his food and looked up above his glasses.

"Geico, online, had an excellent article about the safeties and hazards of driving at night."

His father and mother nodded but continued eating their food. Bret swallowed, adjusted his glasses, and looked around the table.

"Twelve safety tips for driving at night." He continued. "Combating fatigue, avoiding two lanes, using high beams."

He scanned the table. His mom and dad nodded their heads. He looked over at his younger sister. Gene was fifteen, an all-star softball player, a cheerleader, and a grade-A student. Bret looked down and acknowledged that this conversation had little to do with her worldview. She chuckled and texted on her phone, oblivious to the discussion. Mom and Dad didn't care. She was the All-Star. He stood up, adjusted his shirt, and pushed his glasses up.

"I am leaving at about nine."

He looked at his watch and once again scanned the table. His dad looked up and then placed his hand over his mother's hand. The international sign for "Honey, this is serious" in their home. She stopped eating and looked up. He looked down at his watch again. He had found it at a flea market two summers ago and couldn't believe the man at the table only wanted three dollars. It was a classic 1980s Casio CA53W calculator watch. He always wanted one and didn't even care if it worked. It did. There were a few scrapes on it, and the band was very worn, but he stuffed it in his pocket. Bret walked away as if he had won a five-thousand-dollar scratch-off ticket. His friends at school thought he was a dork.

"What year is it, Bret?" they would laugh.

His dad took a breath and studied his son. "If you think you will be okay," He looked at his wife. "Then, please call us every few hours."

Bret's heart skipped.

Approval?

"We don't like this."

That was short-lived.

"But you are 19 now, and we can't baby bird you forever."

He smiled. His mother smiled under weltering eyes.

"Just be safe, Son."

With that, he removed his hand, and they continued eating.

My sister laughed to herself while glaring at her phone. Bret didn't bother saying goodbye to her. She wouldn't even hear him. He picked up his plate and walked into the kitchen. Placing the plate in the empty sink, he turned to scan the room. His first adventure was about to begin. His heart skipped as he took in the old cupboards. Dusty pictures of grandparents he didn't know, the corner nook with sugar and tea dishes. Since he could remember, the old green fridge was a staple in their lives. Shaking his head and adjusting his glasses, he looked at his watch. 7:35.

Time to pack and get things moving, he thought.

He took in the room one last time and exited, climbing the stairs to his bedroom.

Deciding to go was an easy one. Bret liked his family enough, but not enough. To go out and see the world, although a small part of it, was something he had dreamed of doing for as long as he could remember. Scanning the room, Bret caught himself procrastinating, not sure why. Memories played in his mind as he scrambled around to grab items he could not live without on his journey.

Pausing and fixing his glasses, he stood still and thought, *Should I come back?*

It had never occurred to him that he could vanish. Find a new life. Get a neat little job at a beat-down cafe on the edge of a podunk town with an obscure name. What would his family do? His sister would continue for sure. He would become the new drama she would post about on her social garbage accounts. Putting up pretend sad emojis and selfies, "I lost my only brother."

What about Mom and Dad? Publicly, they would morn him, he knew. Privately, they would sit and drink their tea in the kitchen nook, unaffected.

While reading his hunting magazine, Dad would sip, "We told him this would be dangerous."

The local paper would have an article, "Local Boy Vanishes During Summer Road Trip." Placed in the local section under the school stats for the sports team. Nothing fancy.

Looking to his left, he found what he had been searching for: *The Road Trip Book: 1001 Drives of a Lifetime.* He had seen it that same summer as the watch. That flea market was a gold mine. It was pretty worn, but none of the pages were missing, and it was a steal for twenty-five cents. He spent the summer of 2020 reading that book cover to cover and messing with the watch calculator. He stuffed the remainder of the things he needed from his room and took a deep breath—one suitcase. It was amazing what he had managed to squeeze into it. Five pairs of socks, ten shirts, five pairs of jeans, six pairs of underwear, a roll of toilet tissue, a toothbrush, toothpaste, his collection of national geographic field guides, a road map, his cell phone charger, a pair of old tennis shoes and, now, his road trip book. He stuffed a few granola bars in the top zipper, some small Cheez-it snack pouches, and two thousand dollars in a plastic bag. There was an additional five hundred in his wallet. He once read it was advantageous to have your money split up in case of a robbery or you lost your wallet.

Smiling, Bret zipped it all up and sat on the edge of his bed. He looked to his left and stared out the window. Fixing his glasses, he took a deep breath and looked down at his watch. It was 8 pm, almost time to go. It was going to be a long drive to Vermont. Six hours if he stopped only on his planned route and times. He assumed it would be more like seven and a half, with unforeseen issues.

Every television drama, film, and missing person report told the story of the broken-down car, the wrong road scenario, and the folklore that went with them. Bret had a sound vehicle. He had worked all summer at the McDaniels Apple orchard for two years to purchase it. The 2017 Hyundai Elantra SE was pretty. Shiny black with matching gray interior. The paint job, Phantom Black, made him feel like James Bond when he drove it through town. Six-speed automatic, two-wheel drive, and all his. It cost him 14 thousand, even from his local used car lot. The owner, a golf friend of his dad's, promised to take good care of his son, and didn't disappoint. The chances of this car breaking down were slim—one of the main things that relaxed him about this road trip.

Scanning the room one last time, he lay back on his bed and held up his watch, setting the alarm for eight forty-five. As his research told him, the little nap would assist in being alert. He took off his glasses and shut his eyes. He could hear his family downstairs scuffling, cleaning the dinner table, and chattering about something too muffled to make out. He drifted off to sleep peacefully and dreamed about never coming back.

The fog settled, hovering above the ground like a blanket of cotton. Like around his grandma's nativity scene every Christmas. He wanted to touch it, but something seemed dangerous. The fog made the hairs on his neck stand up, like grandma. Bret wasn't sure when he had awakened and walked out to his front yard. Scanning the property, he turned his head faster than his body, looking like an odd marionette. Now facing the road, he saw his car sitting at the end of the driveway, fog engulfing the bottom half. Bret turned to his left and could see the porch of his house. The cotton covered the bottom step, and the house floated above. He shivered and rubbed his left arm with his palm to stop the goosebumps.

Beside the light glow of the living room table lamp, the house looked abandoned. The place looked dead. Standing still, he listened. It made him uneasy when he realized there was nothing but the hum of silence in his ears. No owls, no animals in the bushes scurrying away. No mother or father asking what the hell he was doing out here at what…? He looked down at his wrist to find nothing.

Where was his watch?

He never took it off except to shower or swim. He looked up at his bedroom window on the second floor.

What is going on?

He lifted his hand to his face, rubbed the sleepiness away, and needed to focus. That's when he heard her. It was a faint whisper behind his head. When he dropped his hands and spun around, it had moved further away into the depths of the fog. His eyes widened, trying to let enough light in to see where and who it was coming from.

"Gene?" His voice cracked, and he tried to yell, but his anxiety choked him at the last second. He straightened up and tried to sound more irritated than afraid.

"Gene?" he called a bit louder. He stood in the driveway and began to become irritated. He was leaving at nine, and his sister was playing, what…? Games? Why?

"Gene," he called again, more confident. "Enough. I seriously am not in the mood for your shit."

He never swore around his parents and never at his sister, but it wasn't the time for this behavior. He had to get ready to go. He stood listening again.

"You are making a mistake." A voice passed from behind, the whisper a little clearer now.

Bret turned full circle and began to hike toward the porch. He could break into a run. He didn't know what he would do if his sister popped out of a bush laughing and taking pictures.

"Big News!" her Instagram headline tacked with a laughing emoji. "Bret's a pussy! Will he make it out there on the road? Follow for more! Hashtag Bretsapussy, hashtag family life problems."

As he reached the bottom step, the voice came up to his left ear.

"You are going to see a mistake."

Bret spun around; his heart began to hammer in his chest. The yard was empty, and it was clear to him that his sister had nothing to do with this. He turned, stopped by the shadow of a figure. Bret froze, trying to scream, his voice pushed down into his stomach. The figure seemed to melt into the steps, into the fog. A face jumped out of the figure, contorted in a grimace. Its teeth bled as its tongue whipped in and out of its broken, hinged jaw. The eye sockets were empty. Fog rolled within them, filling the void. The skin dripped from stark white bone, and sinew stretched to meet its weird contortions.

Bret sat up in a sweat, breathing so hard that he put his hand to his chest and tried to steady himself.

Did he scream?

No one rushed into his room to ask, "What in the hell was going on there?" That was the go-to when interrupted during gameshow night, reading time, or any time. They were not concerned about his well-being. Only whether he was up to something so they could complain. As he tried to slow his breathing, he agreed that this was when he, too, wondered, *What the hell was going on in here?*

The room was calm, and his heart was the only thing pulsing in his ears. He strained to listen and decided he would get up and check the hallway. Opening the door, he peered out into the silence. The house and its inhabitants were sleeping. He looked down at his wrist, his watch face glowing a faint pulse. He relaxed at the comfort of it being where he knew it should be. Raising it to his face, he illuminated its square display, closing his eyes with irritation when it reflected 2:30 a.m.

Bret returned to his room and closed the door with a swift slam. He could care less if he shook the whole house awake.

"What in hell is going on here!" His father's voice called through the floorboards.

He would ignore it as always but with a faint smile this time. He fell onto his bed, face down. "You will miss me when I am gone, you miserable old bastard."

Morning, that's when I will leave.

He closed his eyes for the last time, dreaming of safe travel. Not the dark figures with rotting faces that awaited him in death.

The Runner

It was around 6 am when I stopped at the top of Burgin Drive. You know the road. Everyone knows the road. It was everything anyone could talk about for three months. The incident blew through like a tornado and rattled our small town, disrupting what we had built. Safety. Peace. Community. I stopped jogging the route for several months during and after the incident. I couldn't bring myself to look at that house. I knew three of the victims. The other four weren't complete strangers, but I knew the others. It made my skin crawl to see their pictures in the paper. Smiling and happy, not knowing this was how we would last see them. That's a good thing, I suppose. Better than down there, in his cellar. I stood at the top of the hill and watched the fog lift from the asphalt. The swirls lulled me, the phantom dancers rising and diving. My runner's high was beginning to wane. I should have kept moving. I stepped forward, my knees shaking, as I descended the hill before I could think.

Burgin Drive, aka Murder Hill, was a three-mile stretch of road known for two things. One. The perfect place to run due to its seclusion. There was only one residence. And Two. The house itself. It was a two-story, five-bedroom Victorian built in the early 1800s, and it was innocent. Sitting vacant for several years, the locals paid it no mind. He made it evil.

The paper posted no picture, only a vague description of the man. Worn and thin with spiky black hair, a sunken face, and feminine hands. I always thought that was a weird fact, his hands. Joyce Caldwell, the property owner, gave the description. She said she had only met him once, to give him the keys. The rental agreement and application were done online. It's the way things are these days. She commented that being in a hurry that day made it hard to remember his appearance. The man rented the house in July 2009.

I never saw the man as I jogged past the home several times that summer. It surprised me that it was occupied. It always looked so deserted and run-down—no offense, Joyce. The paint chipped and fragmented, white patches of skin that aged and fell away. The windows were dark and lifeless, like sleepy eyes. Vines crawled up the lattice and walls of the home like veins, penetrating the cracks in the wood siding. It was an old soul, but only a house. He was the one who had taken away its innocence. Branding the nickname that would forever haunt that place until its destruction—the Cellar of Hell.

Even Burgin Drive couldn't escape him. I even called it Murder Hill. In the wake of the murders, the stranger vanished. No one slept. I didn't, that was for sure, and the gossip... Everything you could imagine became whispers in the corners of coffee shops. Wide-eyed gasps in lines at the market. Most of the stories were paranoia mixed with the stranger's unknown whereabouts. To these people, it wasn't a matter of whether he would kill again but when.

The soles of my runners slapped against the pavement, and I bounced on my toes, trying to silence the siren. The house would know I was there. My calves burned, lactic acid building, strangling my muscles. Each step pushed the trees back, exposing the edges of the house. I closed my eyes and picked up the pace, ignoring my legs, the twisting in my stomach, and the fight or flight telling me to turn around and go another route. Can't. Like when you see a terrible wreck, neck arching to see the blood. I wanted to see its insides. I needed to. Is that morbid?

I remember the first time they showed pictures inside the house—national news. CNN even had a small piece on our little town. The stranger launched into stardom. The American obsession with serial killers. Was he a serial killer? I would assume so. I don't know the exact definition. The news footage was, in itself, damaging to our town's identity. They were cautious not to hold the camera on the remains. Ugh, that sounds so impersonal. So victimizing. They *were* victims. The video passed over sections of human forms in a blur. I have heard hushed conversations. People recognizing the backs of heads, sprawled arms, and the gaping mouth of one victim, half buried. Although in disbelief, I leaned into the television several times to see if I recognized someone—the morbid fascination. It felt familiar somehow.

I approached the house on my right and tried to look forward. My brain pulled my head,

Look at it.

No, I don't want to. There is nothing there to see.

Yes, you do. Stop pretending. You want to see the inside again—the cellar, what has been done. So, look.

I turned my head and pursed my lips. The house stood at the top of an embankment. The familiar old cement steps, cracked and moss-covered, faded under the shade of a large oak tree. Bushes, unkept, dangled over parts of the walk, obscuring the cracks and weeds. Every step was in slow motion. I must have passed the house by now. It seemed to stretch as my vision bobbed up and down, my breathing heavy, my legs screaming. I forced my eyes to look ahead, assuring I wasn't veering off the shoulder, and then I saw it. Out of the corner of my eye. In a window to the left of the front porch. The shadows and grime danced and created illusions. Yes. That was it. Of course. I stopped and felt my knees buckle. I bent forward and grasped my knees, looking up into the darkness of the porch—his face. A smile in the depths of the shadows and mold on the glass pane. I know, I know. Illusions. I agree and even went so far as telling myself. But I am lying to both of us, I think. I don't know.

I straightened my posture and felt my lower back tighten. I closed my eyes and wiped my brow. When I looked up at the window, the face was gone. It must have sunk back into the depths of the house. We made eye contact. I know I saw him. You know it too. I jogged in place for a few moments, feeling my heartbeat pick up, masking the fear. The house faded as I jogged away. He is here. Still here. I needed to tell someone. The authorities? Joyce? I don't know.

No, we did that once. It turned out badly.

I looked back once as I came to the bottom of the hill, needing to be sure before I stirred up chaos. If I hallucinated that, I would be a laughingstock—a paranoid local stirring up gossip. I headed down the street toward my home.

I need to pass again. See if the face returns. It will. I know it.

I approached the top of Murder Hill the following morning and jogged in place, watching the sun rise and paint the road. Looking at my wristwatch—5:45 am—I took two deep breaths before starting my descent. Again, the trees fell back, exposing the steps leading to the Cellar of Hell.

Go ahead, look.

I slowed to a strut and leaned, stretching my neck, trying to see the porch. My mind began to race with vivid exposures of bodies dragged up those steps. The thumps making my eyes twitch, or was that my runners clopping, trying to slow my pace down the steep incline? I don't know.

I closed my eyes and leaned closer to the television to see the familiar faces. The victims. The gossip among the locals. Secret laughter between disrespectful teens.

Then, there was me, wondering what my insults would be. Besides staring. This dark passion to see him. To know, on a personal level, what he did and to see the Cellar on Murder Hill.

Why does it feel so intimate? Is this what I want? Of course, it is, and he knows it.

I went down the hill and approached the concrete steps, not taking my eyes off the front door. Some of my emotions were fear and excitement, the desire to see that face again. This act felt familiar, and that sent my mind spinning. I found it hard to focus as I found footing on the first step up.

Go ahead. I am waiting. He is waiting.

He is not. You lie.

No. No. But if that helps you forward, then continue with that narrative.

My vision bobbed up and down, the door growing closer as the bushes leaned over me.

I have done this before. I have been here. Why does that feel real?

Because you have. You know each other. You are practically family, you and him.

Lies!

Wouldn't that be convenient?

Why don't you shut your fucking mouth?

Wow. Now, that's no way to talk to yourself, is it?

Am I talking to myself? Why am I talking to myself?

Because you're a fucking nutbag, clearly.

I am sorry. That was mean to say to yourself.

Stop!

Fine, fine. Continue.

When I stepped onto the porch, I noticed that the storm door hung open.

Was it supposed to be?

The hinges looked old but sturdy. The hook inside the door hung, clapping against the frame.

The wind?

Yea, the wind sounds plausible.

Didn't I tell you to shut the fuck up?

Sorry. I was just looking out.

I pulled the storm door open and stared at the big cherry wood entrance. The wood and hardware looked pristine. The storm door had done its job protecting the gatekeeper from the elements. With a trembling hand, I grabbed the knob and squeezed. My heart was pounding and froze when I heard the click. I had to inhale deeply to restart its beat. Dizziness swam across my vision, and I leaned against the door frame, resting my head on my forearm. It gave way, and I fumbled into the foyer, into a familiarity that made my mind swim in horror.

The door creaked shut behind me, and all I could feel was death. The screams climbed from the back of my senses, and I cupped my head, pressing against my ears.

Stop!

It's all you. Why can't you understand this? Don't you recognize any of this?

No. I have never...

Yes, you have. Come on, get serious, you crazy bitch.

I am getting tired of your...

You and me both. Go to the basement and see. If the math doesn't equate, then all is lost, I suppose.

I entered the living room. Somehow mapped out in memory, the space guided me toward the kitchen and then to the basement door.

This was a dream. All of this was some sick, twisted obsession that flowered its birth in my hypnagogic state. Rooting itself in my deep sleep.

That's it. I am dreaming. None of this is real.

Open your eyes, Crazy. Recognize the room?

A cold dampness gripped my naked arms, and I folded them, rubbing as my eyes adjusted. I had somehow been here. The dirt floor crawled into dark corners. Face pareidolia formed from the dim lighting, fighting against deep shadows. I recognized them. They were still here, the tortured souls that could not escape what he had done.

We have done.

What?

We. Us. As in a collective.

I felt my breath hitch. I know there was truth in what the voice— me, I—said.

Ok, slow your roll, Crazy. Let us take this in gradual steps.

Take what?

I turned to find the stairs, already knowing where they were. My heart was going to burst if my mind didn't implode first.

Hey, now, come on. I am trying to save us here.

I spun, facing the room's depth, the faces pulled back, legs sprawling backward. Arms and torsos leaking shadows, melting into the void of their graves.

I don't know what the fuck is happening to me, but all this is a dream. I am dreaming.

Were we dreaming when we strangled your friend, Denise?

I felt my mind slip as memories flooded forward. My hands wrapped around Denise's neck, squeezing as she looked at me in horror. The snap. Her limp body. The dismemberment. The trash bags.

There ya go! Now, you remember.

All of this is insanity.

Ya, well, because you're insane. I mean., the other two girlfriends are on you. It would have been best if we had never told them what happened. I wish I would have been there to stop us from being so stupid, but c'est la vie. They had to go. The others, well, that's just what we do.

The room closed in around me as blood puddles formed within the shadows of the floor. Clicking laughter echoed from its depths. I felt like I was going mad.

I am mad. I am mad. I AM MAD!

Oh, shit, ya. We are.

Shut up!

Wait! What is that?

I looked down at my hand. A light beamed against my feet. I turned my palm, a cellphone, the numbers 9 1 1 in black. It displayed fifteen minutes on a digital timer. A voice emitting something I couldn't comprehend from the speaker.

What the fuck did you do?

My arm raised the device toward my ear, and the voice cleared and echoed.

"Ma'am, we have officers on the way. Please remain calm."

Are you serious?

Light rays followed by loud voices, screaming, shadows dancing, dropping the phone, turning, and raising my hands to shade the light.

"Get on the ground!"

NO! Don't let them. Stop this. Do something.

I felt a heat rise through my crotch into my belly. A wetness rivered my legs, and feces heated my backside, filling my pants. My eyes went blind. White fire. He was here. I could feel him in the room. We were here. We.

I felt my lips part, and what sounded like my voice cooed dry and dead, "Daddy?"

I felt our bodies lunge forward as shouts filled the void.

What the fuck have you done?

The Thin Man

The man across the table didn't strike me as the murdering type. There *is* a type. For example, the ones that can't look you in the eyes. They are sometimes the type. I have a good explanation, but we are not here for that. Just know this guy couldn't look me in the eyes, and he *is* the type. He would look past the right side of my head. His pupils would dilate—extreme mydriasis. The entire sclera would appear black. It was fucking creepy. In truth, I was over my head interviewing this guy, knowing his history. I jumped at the chance during a morning conference. When I lowered my hand, a few colleagues shook their heads, making sure to catch up with me in the breakroom.

Tim grabbed my elbow. "You know who this guy is, right?"

He was a little reserved when picking cases. However, he gave me the heebie-jeebies with how he closed in. He tucked his chin into my neck and whispered. I pulled away and mock-slapped him. I wanted to punch him. I don't like people that close. I lost my nerve when the Thin Man did it, even though handcuffed to the table. That's my nickname for him, the "Thin Man." Nothing unique. He *was* rail thin. If you are not familiar with the term, let me explain. I had picked it up from my Aunt Meridith. My cousin Becky suffered from anorexia.

Aunt Meridith would, in hushed tones, look Becky up and down and say, "God, she is rail thin. Soon she is gonna' disappear if they don't do something."

There were days when I felt that I could see right through her. Like, she would rip if I poked her too hard. The Thin Man reminded me of her sometimes. Not that I didn't like Becky. She was difficult.

I left the office feeling overwhelmed.

Should I have taken the case? No. Does it matter now that I am dead? No.

Chief said no one wanted to be in the same room with that man because his eyes were weird. As I learned, that detail was one of the minor things strange about the Thin Man, like how he killed his wife. The reason was out of this world crazy. It involved a pawn shop, a wedding, a ring, and several accounts of demonic possession.

See? Crazy shit.

The night before my first meeting with him, I couldn't sleep. I kept having visions of him touching me on my forearm. Caressing me. The light shadowed his face, so I could only see his smile—the typical horror movie scene. The room around us fluttered in and out of focus.

Should I call Wes Craven now? Did I steal a scene? I'll wait for the call.

My skin felt wet. No. Clammy. The chains connected to his wrist clanged against the steel table when he leaned across. It made me wince. I don't remember the table being metal. Was it? Ya. His hand felt like fire when his fingers grasped my forearm.

"The secret is the ring, darling. It's the ring."

That's all I remember. Oh, and I peed on the bed. I woke up soaked in the smell of piss. I would say I am embarrassed, but you weren't there. I didn't see the Thin Man's eyes. Thankfully, that came the following day when it was too late to turn around and get the fuck out of there. If I had seen them in my dream, I would have called the whole thing off. I would not have shown up, pleading with the Chief until he gave in and assigned me another case. I would have born the "I told you" and then moved on, of course, giving a sad, "I should have listened" expression. In the past, there were a few cases in which this technique worked. As I stared at the grey metal door, I wondered if I was hard of hearing. Behind that door sat my demise. Behind that door sat the Thin Man, the eyes. Behind that fucking door was the most insane story anyone would ever hear and never believe. In my grave, I still think about him.

I put my papers on the edge of the desk and pulled the wooden chair out. The hard plastic stoppers scraped the floor and made my teeth hurt. That type of sensation always came over me in harsh audio environments.

That was a mouthful.

It's like when my tongue runs over the opening of a straw. My spine stiffens, and anxiety climbs my back like a spider. I can't breathe, but I do it again. I have to. I move the chair and hold my breath. The room feels cold, and I wonder if they do that intentionally. Some weird psycho-analytic thing.

He was blurry when he entered the room, like a fade-in. I squinted to focus, but it wasn't necessary. When the Thin Man approached the table, he looked down in my general direction. There was a gentleness. They do that, too. Psychos. Murderers. His eyes say, "trust me, while his mind says, "So I can bury you in my yard."

Fucking creep.

"My name is Mellisa Jonet," I say.

The Thin Man stares down, his smile straightening until his lips thin into a tight slit. He sits.

"I don't have hours to spend on this case as the FBI has more jurisdiction here than we do."

An FBI officer across the room frowns at me. I pretend not to notice.

"Honestly," I continue, "I think they are just humoring us."

When I looked at the agent, he leaned forward like Michael Jackson in "Smooth Criminal." Now, he knows that I noticed.

I will not share Thin Man's real name because it will not lead to anything good. It's like an omen.

Is that the right word?

It's like a signal. You say his name, and he might show up at your next birthday party. When you're alone on your way to your car at three a.m.

The Thin Man sat down, placed his palms on the table and itched the surface. His eyes never once met mine. Again, he would look to my right as if looking at me would cause me to burst into flames.

Is there any truth in that?

Even as he strangled me, he never once looked into my eyes. I wanted him to. He owed me that. The hours I spent over his story, the details of his wife. The stranger and his wife. Their murders. But I never got it. I blacked out. I was unaware and long dead if he did.

"Did you enjoy it?"

What kind of first question is that? The kind that gets to the point, and Johnny Law over there keeps looking at his watch. So, I was limited.

"Did I enjoy what?" I pretended his words didn't affect me.

"The details of what I did to her."

I remember running that question. Like screaming out of the backseat window in the Lincoln Tunnel.

He sat back, his shoulders slumped. He seemed relaxed and happy.

Of course, he was.

"You have the documents."

His index finger wiggled like a mealworm. I wanted to snip it off and shove it up his ass.

"Yes," my voice felt strained.

There was a shock of an underlying fear that I manifested.

Why?

The bastard was in chains and could do very little harm. I wished beyond whatever higher power you believe in—name it, so you can fill in the narrative—but I knew how much of a lie that was as he strangled me into the darkness.

"I have read the files."

He studied me and then clasped his hands, leaning forward on his elbows. His eyes hovered above his hairy knuckles. He raised his eyebrows and then slammed back into his chair, laughing. The sound made Officer Limp Dick jump, and I looked over, hoping he didn't see me almost piss myself.

I shuffled through the folder. Each page had a crisp edge, like a knife, and I can't say I didn't feel guilty that I wanted to slice his throat, as Officer Opie injected rounds into me as I jumped on the table and splashed in the man's blood.

I slid a page before the Thin Man, and he leaned forward. His eyes scanned the document, and his upper lip curled down, stretching his face.

"It is incorrect."

"How so?"

The blackness of his pupils rolled up and met mine with a burning mockery.

"I had stabbed her thirty times, not twelve, as stated here." He points to the page.

I opened my mouth, and he continued.

"I also had her incinerated so I could have her pressed."

"Pressed?"

He smiled and relaxed in his seat.

"That's why her body remained missing. This twelve-stabbing thing was me reporting in my hazy mindset. You know, after the adrenaline of getting caught."

I had nothing at the moment. I waited and listened.

He smiled.

The prick lived for this reaction. You're welcome.

"I turned my wife into a ring."

"You what?"

He wiggled in his metal chair, trying to redistribute his weight. My ass hurt too.

"I don't follow," I said. "A ring?"

He showed his teeth, folding his arms across his chest.

"ForEverLove."

Hearing the word "love" spit through his teeth sounded wrong, and I could taste it.

"It's a company out of Seattle."

He coughed into the open air. The mist sprayed over the table, disappearing into the reflection of the metal.

I waited. There was a story. Psychos always have a story.

"They take the ashes of a deceased loved one…" he scanned the ceiling as if expecting something to descend upon him. "Is it always a loved one? I am just assuming that." He grinned, scanning the darkness above him. "It certainly wasn't in my case."

I shuffled through the papers, and I assure you there was nothing in the files about a ring. Nothing about ForEverLove, or Seattle.

"After I killed her, I had a buddy. Now, I say 'buddy' in the general sense. He was more of an acquaintance. But aren't we all? Anyway," he continued, "we transformed her into the proper format and delivered her to ForEverLove."

"Format?"

"Let's not dawdle on the particulars of the burning. Just know that was the objective."

I listened, only once looking over at the agent. He flipped through his phone. He was probably looking at underage girls dancing on Instagram or some pervy shit. He was oblivious to our conversation.

"I believe," he pointed to my notes, "there is nothing about the ring's whereabouts. No mention of it at all."

He was right. My expression confirmed it. He nodded.

"I am hungry."

He raised his hands and slammed them on the table. The agent jumped and almost dropped his phone.

"I am hungry," he repeated.

As the agent removed him from the table, he turned, looking into the corner of the room, and paused.

I sat staring, my eyes burning.

"Look up, Connie Odessa."

He became rigid as if time had frozen, a single tear running down my cheek and collecting in the corner of my mouth. My tongue lapped the salt as he faded into the prison halls.

I sat for several minutes, trying to digest it all. I have no idea how long I sat there.

When the agent returned, he looked at me confused and shook his head. I remember him shaking his head as if I didn't belong here in all this. I didn't.

"There is another visit scheduled in ten minutes."

I looked up and nodded. The agent left the room, and I sat there until asked to leave by a fancy lawyer in a shiny blue suit.

I returned the next day after three hours of sleep. My watch said eleven thirty-two. The agent stood in his corner, scrolling through his phone. I had another folder with information about Mrs. Odessa and ForEverLove. The now deceased Mrs. Odessa. ForEverLove, specializes in turning the ashes of deceased loved ones into diamonds. You could put them on a necklace, turn them into a ring, or several other options, all available on their discrete website. All is done through emails and USPS mail.

The Thin Man took his seat and shook his shackles, scanning the room for his invisible onlookers.

"Her husband murdered her." That was my entry into our conversation.

He bobbed his head in confirmation.

They were newlyweds—four months into bliss. The husband, Gary Odessa, bludgeoned her to death with a ball-peen hammer in their living room while watching Family Feud. That detail, in particular, may be nonsense. It was the story that floated around the office.

"What do they have to do with you?"

"Me?" he gawked at his reflection on the metal table. "My wife," he tapped his index finger on his mirror image, "she is the one you need to talk to, if you could ask."

I was too tired for his shit. I remember how my mind floated in the information.

"You are lost, I know." Looking at the agent, then scanning the ceiling again, his voice became soft. The tone was lulling me. "Let me fill in the blanks."

My breath shuddered, and I wanted to sleep. I wish I knew I would be sleeping forever in less than an hour. I would have had a cup of coffee. I would have masturbated before coming here. Smoked some pot.

"After I put my wife down and we obtained the desired format, we sent her off to ForEverLove."

My eyes were so dry. I remember them feeling like sand—the voice like a nursery rhyme.

"The ring ended up pawned by my acquaintance."

I couldn't look at him. I didn't understand what was wrong. I had no idea what he was capable of. It was magic—something about which I could never quite make sense. I tried to speak. Call out to the agent. I listened, trying to moisten my mouth with what saliva I could conjure.

"Have you ever heard of Revenant?"

The voice swished around my skull like a mist. His mouth didn't move.

"It means returning." He smiled. "It's Old French."

I began to cry. I craned my neck, the tendons pulling my shoulder muscles tight. I wanted to scream.

"It is the reanimation of a corpse. I wasn't expecting it, to be honest." He laughed. "She apparently was liked by someone out there in the nether."

I began to gag. My tongue felt like moss, swelling within my throat. I heard a clang, and through my watery slits, I watched as Thin Man stood, his shackles collapsing onto the table.

"With very little diction, I sent her back to the void."

I clenched the armrests as bile rose into my chest.

"They won't be able to explain what happened to you, and that's ok. It isn't meant to be understood."

His form twisted in the shadows of the room. Screams from the agent filled the space. The cracking of bones and ripping wet sounds pinging my eardrums, tearing them. In my silence, he appeared before me, straddling my form.

"She possessed the ring, you see. Genius, really."

Long, warm tendrils wrapped around my throat. I took one shallow breath before they clenched tight. As I choked, vomit rose behind my swollen tongue, and my eyes bulged as I tried to swallow. I could feel my slowing heartbeat as blackness pulsed deeper and deeper until I was blind.

"We were more alike than I would like to think," he laughed.

"Gary purchased the ring and, in his cheap pride, sent his wife and himself to their graves."

I faded into warmth. A cold serenity climbed my limbs, and I became relaxed.

"I envy her." he cooed. "Although we both have our prisons."

The last beat rattled my chest. I could feel everything lift, my chest opened, and the bile dissipated. I was something and nothing. I was everything.

There was a whisper. I couldn't quite make out its origin. I wasn't Thin Man.

"Do you seek revenant?"

I floated quietly within the void.

"Yes."

"Then, take it."

The Trail

The soil smelled foul. Leaves, twigs, and random wood debris cluttered the corpse, hiding its natural features. The earth gave her a mystical look, like something out of a fairy tale. Magical. Her mouth was open, and the soil flooded out, leaving only a few, white, boney teeth shining. It broke the hue of the brown moldy ground. Porcelain skin looked gray in the light. The trees above cast shadows, making her complexion dance along with nature's rhythm. Her hair spread out above her head like a magnificent crown. Queen of the dirt people. Ruler of the dead. The light brown highlights faded into the edges of the soil, painting her into her grave's architecture. The arms extended out, palms up, enjoying the bed.

It was Christ-like, I thought.

Her eyes. Open. Lifeless. She stared at the trees above, studying with curiosity and wonderment. It allowed her to hold the gaze eternal. Exposed to nature, her breasts protruded like giant, supple mushrooms. Her nipples were still pink and hardened from the cold. Her torso was half-buried. The reds and whites, splashes of bone and tissue creating vibrant hues, breaking the mundane browns and greens of the wood. Soil covered her pelvis. Her left leg remained engulfed in the earth and her right leg sprawled above the mound. This mimicked how she would sleep on hot summer nights as I watched her. Peaceful. Here it seemed coupled. I decided to leave her intact as damaging her body would ruin the beauty in the art before me. Pleasuring myself was not an option as it left evidence for essential people of law. But oh, how I desired it. I stood, thinking about her discovery.

Who? What would they think? The first reaction?

I got down on my knees, leaned in next to her face, and closed my eyes. I could smell her skin. Her soft and beautiful makeup covered the scent of the soil. Her tears staining her face smelled of salt. I leaned in and kissed her cheek. I stood, wiping my palms down my pant legs. I scanned the woods. Silence. I smiled down over her, my work, my art. Closing my eyes, I turned and headed back onto the trail. It was going to be a hot day today. The news reported the mid 80's, and she could rest in the cool shade. I needed an iced coffee. It was a beautiful day to walk in the park, to watch the children play, take in the sun—a fine day.

Part 2

IMAGES

Gora

I Died Saturday

Folk

The Runner

The Thin Man

The Trail

Part 3

POESY

Mr. Gehenna

We rock heavily, the dinghy taunting us to the open
mouth of the bay.
My voice was stolen, the witch winds trying to keep my
secret.
I extend my finger port side, my eyes widening.
"It is here!" I shouted.
"I placed carrion in her depths!"

Maniacal Business

Straining to remain in control, forearms stressed,
metacarpi turning a shade of purple.
Blue veins rivered, pulsing in synchronicity with the
maniacal grasp.
The work it takes to strangle another human being is
beyond taxing.
The demand for the follow-through is specific, and the
technique even more so.
The receiver must hold consciousness as close to the
end as possible, ensuring arousal for the antagonist.
Your eyes focused on leaving the now—my excitement
of taking the now joined in one harmonious moment.
As the youngsters say, the struggle is real.
Maintaining the grip until the end, overcoming the
adversity of their fight-back instinct,
holding steady, the end fruitful.
Sitting back, panting, muscles expired,
their gouges and protests concluded in acceptance of
the conclusion.
My tongue left an acrid flow pinched between two
polished cuspids, branding a dedication to the craft.
Throttling is laboring and not to be taken lightly.

Integument

When the flesh is removed, our souls are bare to the ideas of the elements. But our epidermis is a fallacy—nature's joke.

They

It can be a tranquil place.
We stay away from the water's edge in this town.
Waves, like needy puppies, will lap at your toes,
begging you to play.
They are in the deep, and they come from the glaciers.
You cannot escape them once they hold you.

Caterpillar Demon

Papal vestments, unspeakable treason.
Writing our history, naming our seasons.
The right hand is stained red,
The left stands to reason.
Crawling on their bellies, a caterpillar demon.
The scry sweeps the feather and spews tongues with
blank feelings.
Miracles invested, praising angels on ceilings.
Gold lines the coffers, prophets, and deacons,
Witches are gathered, and the heathens are beaten.
Sworn enemy of humanity by the caterpillar demon.
Centuries will pass, the houses of legion.
The voice of the voiceless will strengthen and weaken,
but none shall fool more than the caterpillar demon.

inspired by Paul J. Sister II

Shooter

Your transgressions are mute.
In-formalities hide them with white teeth.
Taking the lives of others isn't an easy burden to carry.
They make it easier on us.
Acronyms on a list we label with truth, but, in the end,
we only pretend to trust their words.
The fictitious wordplay is about the family and the
hardships one has encountered before choosing the act.
Or was it truthful, a heartfelt sentiment that failed to
reach our hearts?
Are we monsters too?
Sympathy is a fad, our discerning list of good-doer
tactics.
We toss the list aside to favor the following perceived
trend if we have opposing thoughts.
Drawing a strike-through like a grocery list of
acceptable jargon.
Are we monsters too?
The story will pass.
We will find another flavor of the day.
Soon, there will be another, and, like the shooter, we
will load up our mental chambers, cocked and ready for
the white teeth to spin a tale.
We will aim.
We will shoot.
We are all monsters.

Aspersing Incident

The air tightens, fingers compressing, strangling the
field of vision.
Features contorted from the strobing glass.
A grimace countenance, my organs of sight ebbing in
conjunction with the tallowed grave.
Gulping like a fish,
Eyes, flitting, mimicking perciforms.
Arms floating tranquil, the grip loosens.
Environment fading spherical, the victory apparent.
Sea tangle silk lulls me to sleep.
Now a statistic.
An ever-rising movement in society.
A Vogue.
My five minutes of fame, a canard.

Road Signs

She felt she could allow herself to cry.
"It's the little things." strangers say.
To let it out.
The tracks run straight through the city.
Like her life, the fences ran through her yard with
flecks of white paint, fading into rust, where the whores
can't hear.
To them, it's just the way of things.
Eyes like those see it all differently.
They truly push it.
But her? Not so much.
She will decide what path when she is ready.
So, until then, she will let some out.
Cry—just a little, where the whores can't hear.

Genesis

I remember Timmy McConald pushing my face into the dirt. That stupid laugh mimicked his older brother, Ronald, who I also hated. The small pebbles scraped away my skin as he pushed against my temple, sliding my face. I could see Becky Caldwell, the girl with the perfect hair that smelled like roses and candy, staring at me with a shame in her eyes that was solely meant for me. Timmy was yelling some insults as spit foamed from the corners of his mouth. His voice was muddled, and my eyes fixated on Becky. Pushing the pain deep into the depths of my stomach, I could hear my breath taste the dirt as it puffed up and recoiled back.

I choked and tried to spit, but my face was compressed by the weight of Timmy's body. I hate Timmy and his fucking family. Sorry mother. She hates unintelligent language. I don't really know what that means, but she lets my father know every time he curses. How do I quiet my mind and wait for the end? I focus on something away, away from this. I think people who have bullies learn this as time goes on. I don't know. With one eye not filled with muddy tears, I stared past Becky and the kids gathering to watch. Past the laughter and stares. I am hypnotized by simplicity.

The merry-go-round with its slightly bent frame, making it wobble out of sync as it turns, alone, like me. The red paint was chipped and damaged. I have never noticed that before. I could hear the metallic squeak, rust trying to grind the machine to a stop. It continues to slowly turn and work. It is rhythmic, and I close my eyes and drift into it. The dirt and sweat, pain and laughter, were gone. The stares are replaced by the vision of the slowly turning merry-go-round behind my eyes. The metallic squeak pulses and calms my breathing into a steady pattern.

When I open my eyes again, Timmy is being marched away by a teacher. The children look wide-eyed at me as Mrs. Mackie, the school nurse, looms over me, making a scene. I can see her mouthing my name, but I lay there and close my eyes, relaxing. I smile, and my body goes limp. I hate Timmy and his fucking family. I just want to smell roses and candy. I realize I hate her too at this moment. We all make mistakes, especially when we are this young. Unfortunately, she didn't have a chance to look back on them. Becky was killed that summer, and I was there. Timmy was too, and I hated him and his family for that too.

It is the reason I kill.

Fierce

The cloud splits, dancing across the sky, a ballet of
lovers, and it seems to sway.
Those who wanted to watch it.
It made Carl look relaxed for a few minutes,
and he felt love.
He looked back down and continued to bury his victim.

That Madness

Am I mad?
"Mad as the hatter, baby!"
I spit.
Did you breathe, raping yourself of dignity?
Then, what's the matter, hatter?
It's those lies, yeah?
It is all in the wrist, she says.
"Well," I quip, "use it to jack me off."
I shut my mouth.
"It is not us that is mad, and I think you begin to realize
this."
I nod, smiling.
"Your way," I say.
"Not mine." she stares.
Mad as the hatter.
Mom was right.
People do have sharp teeth, so I keep my mouth shut.

Jimmy is a Problem Solver

"I have no idea what to do about Becky?"
"What do you guys think?" Jimmy smiles at his glossy-
eyed dog and two hamsters, more interested in the chew
blocks than his dilemma.
"What friends you are." he grumps.
He begins to pace the room, kicking random objects on
the floor, including a TV remote, an empty soda can,
and a crumpled Doritos bag.
Jimmy stops and raises a fist in the air, pointing his
index finger.
"OK," he faces his non-participants.
"We will invite my grandmother and her reading club
for a cookout!"
He began to get excited, pacing again.
"We can eat the rest of Becky!" he raises his hand in a
magician's pose.
Jimmy claps his hands, the slap making his friends
jump.
He points.
"Who doesn't love a good cookout!"

Drip Stain to the Left

Porcelain rimmed with gold, smooth to her lips. Butternut notes danced on her pallet. A drip stain to the left. A thin newspaper, black and white, was glaring. The Headline "Woman Kidnapped from a Local Bank."

She put her cup down and scanned the corner of her thick lashes. Tilting her watch, the hands warn of dawdling; she looks back to the black and white.

"Taken," she mumbles, wincing at the word "kidnapped"—wasn't a kid.

The car would have to be cleaned. Daddy just had it detailed the other day. She should have taken the Subaru.

She needed to leave.

She returns the rim to her lips, mournful she had to abandon the sweet, calming emotion. Gathering her things, she surrendered the black and whites to the next occupant.

Church service is at 12:45, and the hands mock. 10:30, and a hole would need to be dug. That would take a solid hour if her friend showed.

She set the cup down, still warm, and left three dollars, the Washingtons left to stare at the drip stain to the left.

Baby Killer

She was dying.
Men and women are rushing around the room, one of
them holding a baby.
Laying it gently onto cold steel, poked and prodded, she
whimpered.
Turning her head to the side, yawning, her new eyes
could barely make out the silhouette of her dying
mother.
She had killed her, she knew this.
The steel table made her shiver, but she cooed.
"I hope all of my murders are this easy."

Irregularity

"I'll be there at 9!" I arrive at 11, late, from staring into the mirror with false importance. I pass my table, straight for the line to the stalls. Men are busy next to ladies with too much lipstick and little personality.

A deformity. Synonym, Irregularity.

I abandon my position. Holding it for a while is healthy. Pulling back my chair, I scan the table, faces saying 11:15. They are just as annoying as my Rolex.

"So," I say, blank-faced but chipper in tone. "I'll have what Becky is having."

Their faces have a secret I am unaware of until I notice Becky's absence.

"She's not coming," my mother says flatly.

"Surprise, surprise," I return in like tone.

"Well," I smile, showing as little teeth as possible. It's rude.

"I will have what Mother is having."

No one gets my humor. The bitch has no taste.

"She called off the wedding, John."

I nod, unamused, unprovoked, and unfazed.

"I know," I smirk. I didn't.

I stand, turning with a sweep of my open palm, face up. "It's on me," I smile with more teeth. It's rude.

"Tell Becky I said 'Hi.'"

I pull out my phone and walk away, tapping little letters to false friends. I get a return message.

"Kim is here!"

"See you at 12," I return.

I will arrive at 1.

Mother was right when she said, "Mistakes are like sugar."

Once you get the taste, you are hooked. That was my takeaway.

"Hi, Kim." My tone is stale.

I extend my hand. She rolls her eyes.

"Like my Rolex?"

Unwanted

She turns slowly, with faint humming sounds of fluid
strumming over the new vertebrae.
She can feel a limb stretch.
Disruption.
What is that? she wonders.
Louder. Then, more clamorous.
Disruption.
Her eyes cannot see.
What is this sound?
Her chest begins to rattle.
Her last breath is taken without fear but wonderment of
a world she will not know.
You can't fight not being wanted.

When it Ended

This was how.
Everyone knew.
Her toes curled the edges, the wind cooling her legs.
Deep down. Colder still.
This was how everyone knew.

Craving Combat

Skin prickling.
The arm hairs like marines in formation, working into a
frenzy.
The hostess would ramble on, but I was fixated,
passively listening.
My eyes were like saucers, watering, too afraid to miss
the arrival, quivering.
Hot streams released their torture, excusing me without
question using their hospitality.
I am entering the adjacent room and collecting the
nerves, relaxing the soldiers by rubbing the appendages
and taking deep breaths.
The smell, like a bullet, ripped through my narial
cavity, the senses liquid when sauntering into position.
The demitasse sniper.
The hero.
Dying tasted so good.
A ritual.
The black decoction of life.
A pool of immortal calmness, clarity, and rejuvenation
from malaise.
Commander in chief.
A muse.
The Cheshire grin was mistaken for interest in cubical
mysticism.

How are We Doing

The playing fields. Streets.
You are leaving footsteps between your conversations.
"Jimmy, did you bring your gun?"
He is the rooster.
Bright red hood shaded green to prevent the onlookers.
They can see him.
It's my brother, one-hundred children with glowing
eyes, like hens, they follow the rooster.
Cocksure.
We see him.
Head your flock, cock.
"Fuck those taxmen." A hen raises her fist.
His flock is growing, four to ten, ten to twenty, years to
me, but seconds to my brother; he is the rooster.
Grow it until the hens lose count.
That is the state you want to keep them in.
Which one is the mother hen?
The rooster knows.
They see her.

Meat Market

He walks into the room with stark white walls.
A man looks up and pulls his face mask down with a
bloody glove. "Can I help you?" he rests his hands on
the table.
"Why yes!" The visitor pulls out a small, folded paper.
Adjusting his posture, he unfolds it and clears his
throat.
The masked man stares in bewilderment.
"I need three pounds of thigh meat and some tongue if
you have it."
The visitor pauses for an acknowledgment before
continuing.
The worker holds up his finger, interrupting.
"Sir, you do realize this is the coroner's office?"
Looking down, he shows his teeth slightly. Nervous.
"Of course, I do." the visitor replies.

A Pack a Day

Sitting in front of his television,
"Smoking kills thousands a year."
He looks over the rim of his glasses and nods in
agreement.
He bangs the cigarette in the overflowing ashtray and
fixes his stare on his manual.
How to Become a Successful Serial Killer.

Jim

Did you see that man pull out his cock?
That's Miami, Woman!
Bathroom vocals and trashing the hotel rooms.
Get with it, Jim.
Brilliance is backed to the bone with brilliance.
He's with it. Get with it, Jim.
Writers of the chord, Riders on the Storm, and Light
My Fire, with 5 to 1.
His eyes have seen you.
What was Father killers? Mother fuckers?
Did you see Jim pull out his cock?
It was the Lizard King.

7 Dishes

Seven Dishes
He eats while he sings.
He slurps, chews, drinking like a king.
His maids turn with shaking lips.
He snaps a bone.
He is nibbling sinew, pulling meat from his teeth with
greasy fingertips.
His maids turn with shaking lips.
He swallows and clears his throat.
"Have you not seen this cannibal eat before?"

Livin'

How many horrid sins must I carry?
Depending on the minute,
the number may vary.

Sins have titles like the surnames of men.

I hold too many titles.

What should I do then?

The priest calls out a name,
and I'm sure to come running.

But what's the sense of living if you can't have any fun
and
Live as you see fit.

Meant

Is it the way the stars are lying?
Always brighter on the other side and,
Is it fear that's got me thinking,
We were never meant to be this forgiving.

I won't slide
Along for the ride
To feel worse alone
Your heart was once called my home.

If Indeed We Ever Were

Our commonality is a pretense to truth as factual as
one's beliefs.
So how do we, as a reality, deal with intrusion into our
four-dimensional existence?
Can another truth curve reality, bending the fabric of
time to exclude your carbon footprint?
The galaxies within multitudes of galaxies are open to
all possibilities.
Its representation is visible in our irises.
They are cheap imitations of our galactic mothers, void
of its true beauty and omniscience.
We are inherent only in our imaginations, and our
imaginations are inherent only in the rules of an
undetermined plot line.
The question is whether we are overused tropes in the
time spectrum, or are we a rough draft needing edits?
We only need to change the narrative to coax a truth.
If indeed it ever was a truth to begin with.

Fervor

Gravel, like teeth, carrion in its depths.
My arrival, in the lurch, emotion bereft.
Ocular counter in the arrival of a stranger.
The disservice previous, gratis of danger.
Passing, I stare, passing I ponder.
Will dandelions grow where she lay asunder?
Shovel of silver, peppered in red.
My victim, in fragments, lacked her head.
Onward the journey in the field of lamentable.
My hyper-fixation purported unpreventable.

A Killer Among You

The only reason you are safe is because I like to go on walks.
Long walks.
Walks that allow hours of self-reflection with beautiful sunny skies.
Sometimes, sunsets with the distant smell of campfires or backyard
nonsense.
Walks that allow me to stretch my legs and feel healthy.
Walks that are taken from pure freedom.
This is a value, amongst all others, that I indulge in because I am a
law-abiding citizen—wink, wink—and the only reason you are not
rotting away in some ditch or being prodded by a coroner to figure
your demise.
Walks.
You would think it is such a thin line to draw between that which
makes you safe and that which makes you unsafe.
Not really.
On my walks, I pass several people.
My thoughts are always the same, yet each person is guarded with the
safety net of my freedom and the bliss in knowing I have these walks
to look forward to.
To enjoy.
To be at peace.
Walks.

How I Knew

It was that in which I prevailed.
The others faltered.
My reaction was silenced by men I couldn't understand
in a voice I could.
They told me to hush my tone.
I followed.
This is how I knew my voice was lost.
They commended me, but I was not to be remembered.
With that, I understood my mistakes.
They were what made me what I am today.
Not the man I wanted to be.
It's how I knew.

Duology (Irregularity Series Part 2)

The buttons look stoic, sticking slightly, quite dysfunctional. Tonguing the bills, groaning, spitting them pendulously.

John snatches them and checks his Rolex. His mental agenda says 2 pm. Pausing…

She can wait.

He arrives at 3:15.

Becky, he ideates, would dislike any promptness from him. How else could she fuel the complaint train? Thoughts of dinner the other night, guests unamused, showing their teeth. The bill paid, but respect unsettled.

Pushing back his chair, "I'll have what she's having."

He eyes the waiter.

"Not eating," she says, face averted.

Prickly, the waiter backs away. Glare locked onto her, John raises his hand and extends his pointer finger.

"Platinum Passion."

$1,500, a New York thing.

Long pause.

The waiter checks his notes.

John lowers his gaze to the table and swallows.

"Sapphire Martini,"

$3000.

"And box the earrings." He wags his finger, his gaze now circumventing.

The waiter escapes as John checks his Rolex.

They apply their eyes to each other.

*Fuck you, John! i*s not what he hears.

What is this, John? is what he sees.

"Mother seemed amused by your antics."

Her, now staring. Him, jaw slightly clenched.

Her: "You sent her into the fray."

Him: "You or me, I guess."

Her: "Not my sword."

A glass clanks.

Ignoring the deliverer, juniper and citrus itch his olfactory receptors.

Shit.

He holds his position.

"Well, if today hasn't already proved enough chaos…"

Him: "Mother?"

His neck turns at an unnatural angle.

Becky: "You or me, John."

Revenant

The ground recoiled, her arms protruded like roots,
and soiled hair matted against her sunken dermal.

The eyes jutted, frantic as they searched,
her body writhing from beneath the earth.

I sat motionlessly, my mouth and nostrils,
giving away my position, my breath visual in the
moonlight.

She turned, soulless eyes searching, the torso facing
away,
a crack filling the air, her neck adjusting to the
unnatural position of her head.

I gasped.

The mouth of the ghoulish thing opened broad,
rotten dental work falling like decaying seeds.

"I have come for you." It gurgled, pointing its skinless
finger, its eyes jetting left to right.

I held my breath.

There is no escaping what I have done.
She had come, and rightfully so.

Violently Resplendent

It was the face.
The darkness of the room,
Stark against the pools of his eyes.

Those pools.

Curves forming rivulets, running to the corners of its
mouth,
forming a vast ocean of moans and summons.

It was that face.

Empty darkness surrounded it,
so, my stare could distress on nothing else.

I was happy to die just then.
Escaping the visage.

Sheep Dog

Cattle cutter, mincing meanings behind accusations in a
crowd of strangers.
Mental clutter filed deep in a dewy decimal of rotting
lined manila paper.
Pinpoint iris, screaming sirens, and brain on fire with
fear.
I hate rubbing shoulders.
Spittle collecting on the fat lip of an overzealous
storyteller. I think his name is Nicholas.
I detest every word that pours from his insipid mouth.
The herd shifts as the boisterous man circles the left
edge of the playing field.
A cattle driver for sure.
Who is the sheepdog?
I laugh as I see my reflection in a passing mirror.

Compulsory

I pace my apartment,
Wearing the track from the edge of my kitchen to the
couch. Thinner.
The fibers danced, mocking the diligence of creating
my perfect environment.
I need to remove the vile thing.
I grit my teeth at what lies underneath.
I could cut the dances. Create perfection from
something so damaged.
No. No. It would never be, and like the filthy rug, the
corpse of the lady in the bathroom could never reach
cleanliness.
I cut and cut and yet, perfection is lost.
When I saw her in front of the Chinese restaurant on
16th and Fermont St.
I knew there was no ignoring the filth. The way she
licked her lips at me. I felt the sweat under my latex
gloves, I needed to wash my hands.
It had been several days and yet the rot could not be cut
away.
I am scared to enter the bathroom, the red splashes
upon my once pristine bone tooth tile.
So, I leave the door closed until my anxiety dissipates.
So, I will pace the path. I need to cut the dances.

The Red Wonderful

Peppered iron drips known as the red wonderful.
It is taken without remorse as it is, to those who acquire
it, in high demand.
A need more so.
Those who are not in the know are never to be and
present the red wonderful to those of us who are.
We are selected.
The most secret of societies but known to the world
through fables passed down.
Warnings to seekers of the wicked.
Our names penned in the book of the dammed,
quilled with the red wonderful.
When we feed, we thrive.
When we thrive, feed.
Ouroboros in nature,
We create legion.
All hail the red wonderful.

Run, Just Run

My legs ached. The lactic acid tightened my muscles
and I want to pinch my calfskin in frustration.
But I can't stop.
Ahead there is an incline, face down, slightly, and it
will help me hurry.
It wasn't the race.
I was in that godforsaken house.
You know the one.
It has been emptied for some time.
The dungeon is sealed from eating people alive.
The owner, now facing the wall, ironically, in a
dungeon of his own creation by the state.
I pick up the pace as I ascend.
My heart races.
The pumping thudded my brain.
I began to pant.
I swing my arms forward and quicken my steps.
It burns.
I try to look ahead as I pass the structure.
But I can't. I must. I look.
From the upper window, I swear to the life of my
children, I see a face.
Blank deep-set eyes. Fear.
I gasp and I feel my heart will give, leaving me spoiled
on the road.
So, I run, just run.

Free

The rules are regulated to keep the ideas of society safe.
Safe is a safe word.
A fallacy with a fact label, *sans* safe.
Only radical thought processes contradict the norm of
safety.
So, you are a prisoner. We are prisons of ourselves.
Safety does not equal freedom.
Free shall be forever equated with shackles or norms
transfixed into coffee table conversations with bitter
liquids masked by sweet sentiments.

How We Work

It is the way their skin peels.
That gives me the feels.
The way the knife glides,
But, really, that's beside
The point.

Have you ever listened to a human scream,
The fear that accompanies the dream?
The dream that gave me purpose.
To expel what real hurt is.

Is it demons that reside,
My mindset collides.
With the gift, the world has given me.

I will be thankful in a way.
That maybe, just maybe, someday,
This evil will be as silent as it can be.

What Keeps Me Up at Night

The legs.
So many legs that sprawl like tendrils from beneath my
bed, from inside.
The cool sheets brush my body, and my skin responds
with hardened bumps and stiff hair.
My dead parents holding hands in the corner, lurking by
the library door.
Those words aren't yours to take from me, you have
taken enough already.
My spouse, who looks like a stranger in the depths of
our bed, breathes steadily, unaware of my persistent
stare.
She is beautiful but will leave me one way or another.
Probably one way.
The window nearest the AC unit rattles, its bones
warning me that I need to stay inside.
Out there, out there, is us, where the mold grows.
This is what keeps me up at night.

Dear Boss: As We Continue

I have taken my time, Dear Reader.

The state of my mental stability may be in question, but I ask you,

Did I leave her body unapproachable?

Did I not reaffix the bundles of cloth that hid my work, her new form?

Did you not, in your state of authority, look upon her in disdain for her occupation?

What a world we live in, Dear Sir.

I have stood amongst the trill and watched as you fumbled.

The squalor and state of Whitechapel have truly been, at the very least, my protector.

I shall cut again. And again.

There will be no shortness of offense by my hand, and I shall keep you busy during your keep.

Let us be joyful that we have this time together.

Truly.

Your friend,
Jack

Swine

The bareback stomps of brittle toes.
The squeals of demons, moistened snouts.

A fence, the edge where darkness grows,
Ashamed and scorned by Christian doubts.

Black pin eyes, softly weeping,
And to them who came to cross their chest.
The smell of grass and essence seeping,
Suckle upon their mother's breast.

In shadows, the devils wait.
There is no God here, wept the farmer.
It is the sacrifice that will set you free.

Meet Virginia

The coal mines examined through fables that once
played major roles in the backbone of the hills.
These families stage the narrative that embodies the
region.
Meet Virginia.

Black lung shapes the vocal twang of the elders, lost to
youth, and replaced with a southern drawl more
reminiscent of comedy acts.
Meet Virginia.

Sounds of 5 string scrugs and hymnals deep in the
wood, barefoot with child, and set back away from a
society of electronic gods. They raise their young on
breastmilk and folklore.
Meet Virginia.

Documentaries on common life, created as awe-struck
fantasies of our early existence, squint an eye in
wonderment at the prose painted of their mundane
lives.
Meet Virginia.

Feeding

I peeled the skin back so I could see him.
Really see him.
My first impression was common because he was that.
But would that make me feel bad for devouring him?
No.
I remember vague conversations, mumblings, really, of
his family, mentioning his wife and children in passing
tones.
I questioned that.
He tasted single.
I took him for more of the begging type.
Not once did he.
As I chewed on his ring finger knuckle, the first, he lay,
his head lobbed in acceptance.
Later, he bled upon my kitchen floor as I stood above
him, hugging my grinder close to my chest.
I decided, in my rest, that his meat needed garlic.
Well, I needed him to taste as if he were mine.
Placing the grinder on the linoleum floor, it rocked on
its edge before jerking to a stop erect.
I stood staring.
I felt my weight rock as the room began to swell.
My knees ached.
Hobbling to the counter, I rested my lower back against
its sharp edge.
He faded to my peripheral vision as I wiped my maw
on my sleeve.
I need to think about his family.
I kick the pepper grinder.

The Beach

I hated that beach.
The day my toes sank within its soft embrace,
I hated it so.
I was five.
It was ageless.
I refer to it as a living entity because it is.
It surely is.
We knew it was alive when it sank its teeth into my
brother, the blood pooling into tiny gaps in footprints.
It's empty.
Clear of debris or life, now.
The long stretch of round and beautiful pebbles coaxed
its victims into the sun.
Into its void.
Teeth clawed the shore, dragging back tiny round
victims, swallowing its children.
The population of the beach lessened by the second.
So, why has it not died?
I still have dreams of my sister, reaching above the
mouth of the shore as I stood in another world.
I no longer visit, but in my slumber, my sister within its
mouth, my brother's crimson prints upon the sand,
leading me to the mouth.
It is a warning.
I was five.
It was ageless.

Acknowledgments

I have struggled for some time with printing my poetry and short stories. I used these short works for experimental reasons and exercises to draw the imagination and oil the machine. I am forever thankful to my colleagues and friends who pushed me to revisit these stories, build on them, and show them to the world.

I would like to say "thank you" to Aurynanya for being an amazing friend and poetic mentor, yelling, "Shut up, dude! You got this." FYI, your cat Toby likes me more. The proof is in the photo, and I have it.

Margot, my publisher, for believing in my work and in me. Also, thank you for putting up with my nonsense and exhaustive edits. You are a saint.

To Doodleslice for being an inspiration, driving me to explore poetry, and not be afraid to have fun.

Sean Stevens, for being a brother in writing and more so in life. Mr. Remoraman, we have had some wild discussions, and you have read my work in its raw state. Thank you for mentoring me and never holding back.

Steve Yeo, for always pushing me to try out new things. I still don't think tea beats coffee.

To Mt Pariti and Spicy for ensuring the spoken word is for those who have something to say. Spicy, we never did go to Parsnips.

To my amazing wife and children, you always stood by my decisions and obsessive ventures, letting me do what needed to be done to shut me up. I love you endlessly.

Last, but not least, my uncle Eric. You believed in me the most. Mentored me as a child and showed me that no matter what people may say, I could be whatever I chose to be. I just needed to believe and work. You are gone now but always on my mind. It is because of you that I continue to believe. Rest well, I love you.

About the Author

Daegal

Ohio resident and collector of dark words. A storyteller for the unusual and malevolent reader. A spinner of blood and a path for the wicked heart.

Contact Daegal at:

Facebook:
https://www.facebook.com/horrorbydaegal

Instagram:
https://instagram.com/horrorbydaegal

Other Publications Available from Castle Carrington Publishing

Perceptions Press
ESTD 1992

CASTLE CARRINGTON
ESTD 2017

TRANSGENDER PUBLISHING

ALL GENDERS PRESS

Now Available from Castle Carrington Publishing
You have a story. Let us help you tell it.
https://castlecarringtonpublishing.ca/

Pig Heads (2023)
Daegal
Peter Crimth is a killer, and undisclosed disposal of the bodies is paramount. In a small California town, secrets can become urban legends, and Jimmie Pratt, a local pig farmer, keeps the darkest of them. The local Sheriff, Kenneth Burgrin, has little expectations and likes it that way. Knowing more about Jimmie than he would like, he soon learns monsters come in different shapes and sizes.
(https://castlecarringtonpublishing.ca/pig-heads/)

Bingo (2023)
Daegal
Small town Ohio. A boy with a dog's name. A series of family murders. The chief of police with blood on his hands, and the redemption of three souls.
(https://castlecarringtonpublishing.ca/bingo/)

Zombies are People, Too (2023)
DAEGAL
(A children's book)
Are you scared of zombies? Have you ever talked to one They are not much different than me or you. They enjoy eating (no, not brains), playing video games, and making new friends! Because Zombies are people, too.
(https://castlecarringtonpublishing.ca/zombies-are-people-too/)

Good Night, My Child (2023)
S. Stevens
(A children's book)
Good Night, My Child is a reassuring tale explaining what happens when those pesky nightmares come to our children at night!
As parents, we can all relate to those moments when our children wake up abruptly, sad and upset. When they seek our comfort how do we help them best?
Experience and imagination can never lead us astray.
"See we were young too, also had dreams."
Travel with the author during these important moments. How can we make the most impactful statements during one of the most vulnerable times of our children's lives? Let's journey on a mission together to destroy those dreams!
Goodnight, My Child delivers a feel-good way to process those moments and rest easy, once and for all! (https://castlecarringtonpublishing.ca/good-night-my-child/)

Queenie Escapes (2023
Steven J. Yeo
15-year-old Princess Alexandria is an adrenaline junkie, but the palace guard stops her from her from enjoying the dangerous sports she loves. So, she decides to escape her life to be free. But it doesn't quite go to plan.
https://castlecarringtonpublishing.ca/queenie-escapes/

Queenie in France (2023)
Adventures of a Secret Agent Princess
Steven J. Yeo
Representing Edenland at the national speed climbing championships is a dream for Queenie. But Interpol, the Russians, and the Man from Tripoli, all have other ideas. Queenie is soon embroiled into a web of espionage that threatens her chances of competing.
(https://castlecarringtonpublishing.ca/queenie-in-france/)

My Heart is Out for Blood (2023)
Aurynanya
Aurynanya's daring poetry collection *My Heart is Out for Blood* takes readers on a mind-bending journey of madness and intimate triumph. Where there is elegant beauty, there is blood and sinew, where there is trauma, there is healing. Aurynanya cuts herself open to ask the question: "What does it mean to listen to your heart?" Poems of death, survival, and sacrifice are brought to stunning clarity through beautiful artwork. *My Heart is Out for Blood* is a dangerous and thought-provoking collection, relentless in its quest to burrow under your skin and sink its teeth into your very heart. (https://castlecarringtonpublishing.ca/my-heart-is-out-for-blood/)

My Dog Rigby: Just Like Me (2021)
Jan Olsson
My Dog Rigby, Just Like Me explores how we react to our dogs, and what this ultimately reveals to us about the way we treat others.

The approach we use to train and connect with our dogs can provide us with insights about how we can enhance our relationships with our partner, children, extended family members, friends, and co-workers.

My Dog Rigby shares personal short stories that everyone can relate to, focusing on themes shared by dogs and their owners, such as anxiety, capacity, aggression, trust, self-regulation, and patterning within the brain. While also giving practical training tips and advice, this book attempts to reveal who we are, who our dogs are, and the ways we are similar.
(https://castlecarringtonpublishing.ca/my-dog-rigby/)

Pushing the Boundaries!
How to Get More Out of Life (2021)
Peter Jennings

Pushing The Boundaries! How To Get More Out Of Make Life features profiles of 32 people from around the world (many of whom are well-known and featuring many Canadians) who reveal how they triumph in life. We're talking people who have overcome uneasiness about taking risks, like daredevil Nik Wallenda; doctor-of-change, Patch Adams; intersex supermodel, Hanne Gaby Odielle; international clothing designer, Tommy Hilfiger. Also included are Canadians like Marina Nemat, who defied certain execution in her teens at Evin prison in Tehran; McDonald's of Canada Chair, George Cohon, who persevered through 14 years to break into the Russian market; Rick Hansen, who pushed himself around the world in a wheelchair to raise awareness of people with disabilities; Katie Taylor who's broken the glass ceiling by becoming the first female Chair of a major Canadian Bank; Donald Ziraldo, who put Inniskillin Winery on the map by making Icewine into an immensely popular beverage worldwide; etc. As Jack Canfield, renowned co-author of the *Chicken Soup For The Soul*® series says in the book's Foreword, "Having the conviction to reach beyond your fears and take chances means you're ready to achieve lasting success."
(https://castlecarringtonpublishing.ca/pushing-the-boundaries/)

Until I Smile at You (2020)
How one girl's heartbreak electrified Frank Sinatra's fame!
Peter Jennings with Tom Sandler

It's 1936. Take Ina Ray Hutton, the "Blonde Bombshell of Rhythm," add 22-year-old Ruth Lowe, who become Ina Ray's pianist. Ruth marries music publicist Harold Cohen, but he dies in the midst of debilitating surgery. Ruth is devastated, full of heartache, a grief-stricken widow far too early. Consumed by anguish, she pours her heartache into a lamenting anthem that becomes an internationally famous song—"I'll Never Smile Again"—destined to electrify the career of 25-year-old vocalist Francis Albert Sinatra. Ruth next composes what becomes Sinatra's theme song, "Put Your Dreams Away." And then, Act Two begins for Ruth Lowe: she withdraws from the limelight to become a caring wife, loving mother, society doyenne, and friend to many. Amazingly, this superstar has escaped the investigation and adoration that her life so richly deserves—until now.
(https://castlecarringtonpublishing.ca/until-i-smile-at-you/)

Ruth's Wonderful Song: A Story for Kids (2021)
Peter Jennings
Ruth's Wonderful Song is a true story of a young woman who loved to play her bright yellow piano. She wrote a wonderful song that people are still listening to more than 80 years after she wrote it. Tom, Ruth's son, tells the story of how Ruth wrote her wonderful song and what happened next.
(https://castlecarringtonpublishing.ca/ruths-wonderful-song/)

Coming in 2024/2025 from Castle Carrington Publishing
https://transgenderpublishing.ca/

PUBLICATION EXPECTED IN 2024
Queenie in England
Steven J. Yeo
Thrust into the world of espionage and championship speed climbing, Queenie must defeat the "man from Tripoli" and still qualify to win. All the while she discovers that the British do things differently.
(https://castlecarringtonpublishing.ca/queenie-in-england/)

PUBLICATION EXPECTED IN 2024
LOST & FOUND ANTHOLOGY
Edited by Aurynanya
An innovative anthology that showcases diverse works of poetry and art from people all over the world who are on a personal journey of healing. These bold voices have shared their experiences in an effort to normalize the everyday struggles of mental health and provide for those still struggling a safe passage from the darkness into the light.

Starting from one side of this book, readers will be taken on an odyssey of desperation acknowledging the raw and ugly side of mental illness and how it affects us. From the other side, readers will walk a road through experiences of transformation, self-care, and hope.

Lost & Found is a demonstration of what a community can achieve through combining their voices for one purpose: to express that we are not alone.
(https://castlecarringtonpublishing.ca/lost-found/)

PUBLICATION EXPECTED IN 2024
The 27 Club Anthology Project
Edited by Aurynanya
An edited anthology of poetry and art that celebrates the lives of those musicians, artists, actors, and other celebrities who died at the age of 27.

(https://castlecarringtonpublishing.ca/27-club/)

PUBLICATION EXPECTED IN 2024
Being Happy Matters
Peter Jennings
Being Happy Matters is a re-launch of a previously published book *Why Being Happy Matters.* The updated Introduction references COVID-19 and how happiness can be an antidote to the stress and anxiety people are experiencing right now. The original volume presents interviews with people in Canada, the U.S., Asia, Europe, and Australia, each of whom reveal what happiness means to them and why it matters.
Readers will meet international PhDs who are actively studying the science of positive psychology (i.e., happiness). This book features Peter Jennings in conversation with 37 intriguing individuals, including John Robbins, heir of the Baskin Robbins empire (who tells Peter about turning down his inheritance and then losing his life's savings in the Bernie Madoff scandal, but still exhibiting a positive outlook of happy perseverance to life's reversals); Roko Belic, California-based Oscar-nominated director of the award-winning film "Happy"; Dr. Christine Carter, sociologist and positive psychology specialist at Berkeley University ; Rolling Stones keyboardist Chuck Leavell (who shared with Peter the joy he gets from working with his buddy former President Jimmy Carter on key environmental issues); Major League Baseball legend Shawn Green; celebrated super-model & businesswoman Monika Schnarre; Time magazine humour columnist Joel Stein; 84 year old Playboy cartoonist Doug Sneyd; Leo Bormans from Belgium, author of the respected "World Book of Happiness"(who explains what lies behind his discussions with global experts); and much more.
(https://castlecarringtonpublishing.ca/being-happy-matters/)

Publications from Other Divisions of Perceptions Press:

Perceptions Press www.perceptionspress.ca
Stephanie Castle Publications www.stephaniecastle.ca
TransGender Publishing www.transgenderpublishing.ca
All Genders Press www.allgenderspress.ca

www.ingramcontent.com/pod-product-compliance
Lightning Source LLC
Chambersburg PA
CBHW041754010726
47507CB00009B/386